VENOANS A SERIES OF SHORT STORIES

Adam Adams

**VENOANS
A SERIES OF SHORT STORIES**

First Edition: 2022

ISBN: 9781524318215
ISBN eBook: 9781524328207

© of the text:
   Adam Adams

© Layout, design and production of this edition: 2022 EBL

*For Choyce,
as I, your father, bare my soul.*

Table of Contents

Author's Arbitrary Quote

Always ask someone why they're writing, reading, watching, or listening to certain things because their answer may oppose your assumptions.

"On this day, it's so real to me. Everything has come alive. Another chance to chase a dream, another chance to feel alive."

—Myles Turner
& Mark Tremonti

One night in the dark, a vision of someone I know. Out of that darkness, I heard a voice say, "I'm you."

—Jim Johnston

"Stars aligned, new strands of light form in the sky. Now, in this moment, watch the moon eclipse the sun as the blood begins to run."

—Greg Wattenberg, Thomas Saltman,
Mike Lauri, & John Alicastro

Story 1
The Bass Boys

Part 1: Offer

Man was walking home from a stroll around Venoa Lakes.

"Turn it up!" he shouted, as the boys drove up.

"Just for you, old man!" one blurted back.

"What's that *boom* sound?!"

As the driver sped off with the tread skidding against the road, they yelled, "Bass!" and papers flew from the car window. With one folded in his pocket, Man placed them in his recycling bin and walked inside singing.

"Dad, are you alright?" asked Pickney on the stairs with Tucker in her arms.

"Find my glasses, will you?" he asked, stumbling over an old turntable on the living room floor. Pickney scurried over wiping the lenses after he landed on the sofa.

"Dinner's ready," she said.

"Good, I'm starved," said Man, reading. "This seems to be an invitation."

"Well, what does it say?"

"Apparently, there's a party to happen."

She shook her hips saying, "You know I love a good party, dad, where I can dance and stuff! Will you let me see?"

"Now, hold on, I'm thinking."

"*You're* not thinking of going, are you?"

"So, you don't think your old man's hip enough, huh? Don't let the orthopedic shoes fool you. I'm a Black man with more bounce than a hip hop beat," he said, and handed her the flier. "Hang that up on the fridge for me, dear, will you?" Pickney stood there reading it before laughing to herself. "What in the name of Pickney is so amusing?"

"Dad, this is a teenager's party," she said. "School's out!"

He slid out his shoes and said, "I know, but I've got a plan," following her into the kitchen while doing karate movements with his hands. Pickney ignored her father by reminding him of his recent retirement payout. While serving him a large portion of poultry with sweet potatoes and a steaming pile of greens, she told him she met with the bank's Tall Tom at his house in the neighborhood. The teller, who stole money for a Montessori and strode out Venoa Beach Jail for brunch with Judge Brad, advised her. He told her about stocks, bonds, and other ways to invest without the stress of starting a small business like her father did. With her newest expertise, Pickney assumed she could multiply Man's excess retirement money by the time Tucker began talking.

"Are you listening to me?"

"Mmhm," he replied, washing dishes while watching Lady of Red out the window. She watered her plants wearing a wisteria-colored dress with her red hair down with a matching head piece. Her skin was white like the pearls around her neck as she aged like yarrow.

Pickney saw him staring and said, "You're drooling, old man," relieving him of dish duty. Man removed the flier pocketing the magnet and eased his way out the front door. She watched him through the window as he tucked his shirt and wiped his bare face with his moist hands, dabbing his cheeks with a handkerchief. He stood at the house where Lady of Red was with a hose at her toes clearing his throat.

"Well, aren't you going to say something?" asked Lady of Red, turning the faucet.

"Pardon my attire," he said, and removed his baseball cap. "I would've put on my best suit had I remembered how lovely you are."

"How could you forget?"

He gulped and said, "I'm getting older, I guess."

"Now that I've refreshed your memory," she checked the nozzle, "would you mind telling me why you're standing on my grass before I water my roses?"

"To offer you your youth back in return for my own," said Man, and handed her the flier.

She read and laughed, "A teenage girl's house party in Venoa Preserve? What makes you think I won't leave you for a younger man wandering a cul-de-sac without an invitation?"

"Well, I'm known for treating women like a precious gem," he assured her, "like the kind I'm sure to have seen you wear."

"Well," she stopped watering the bush, "with that being said, aren't you going to formally ask me to be your date to this party?"

"There is no better privilege other than Pickney and her sweet potatoes that would give me great pleasure than to do so," said Man, before bending his knee. Lady of Red reached in her pocket for lipstick and applied it while batting her eyes.

With pouting red lips, she smelled the roses, smiled, and held out her hand to say, "I'm ready."

"Will you do me the honor?"

"Yes," she scratched her head, "but I'm curious about why we have to go to this party to feel young again?"

"Because," said Man, standing tall like Tall Tom, "the boys will be there."

Part 2: Boys

The school bell rang as Blake slept with an open water bottle filled with beer he stole from his stepfather's man cave on his desk. The other boys walked in to remind him school was out by easing their way into shouting in his ear. They were an imposing, powerful, thin-pocketed pack with promise, who spent more dollars on digital files than females did to get dolled up. Blake led them through another year as sophomores still doing homework before class began. He was a tall white boy with boulders for shoulders and legs like tree branches in Venoa Beach, who stood with a proud stance always with his hands in his pockets. Fish was fair-skinned with curls that made shy girls follow him down the hall hoping he would turn around. He wore his backpack on his chest and chewed gum like an entree served at

Al's Eatery near Lily's Greenhouse off State Road 1. Haywood and Big Ant were the boldest of the bunch. They were two Black boys with a bearing to brag about the babes who bought them school lunch for packing a punch for punks who insulted them. Haywood was nicknamed "Hero" by Venoa Beach High girls and roamed the halls with Big Ant behind him at six feet six, yo-yoing to the bass that boomed in his head. As the four friends stood by Fish's car in the school parking lot, girls on their way home shouted their names before reminding them of the party.

Fish shouted back, "Bring a friend!"

"Bring a friend?" asked Haywood.

"Cute girls know other cute girls. It's science," he said.

"What if she brings a guy friend?"

"Umm..."

"Don't pay him any attention, man," said Big Ant, yo-yoing against the hood. "His nose is up ever since he lost his virginity to Messy Molly!"

"Tell them, Fish, you learned a thing or two about women since freshman year," said Blake.

"Women? These are girls," he said, tossing his backpack in the trunk with the others.

"Hey, watch those sub-woofers."

"But what's really the difference between a girl and a woman?" asked Haywood.

"Man, haven't you seen Lady of Red? Now, that's a woman," said Big Ant.

Fish asked, "Didn't she pretend to be Ms. Lily?" as more students scattered outside the building. Fish turned up the music always with the bass above treble and an open trunk. While some girls danced where they stood, waving at the four boys, Bobby and The Bang Busters from Venoa Farms drove past.

"Bang!" Bobby shouted out the window of his custom pickup. He was seated high with a suspension lift kit holding them up on oversized tires. The other two boys stood in the cargo bed shouting out their best pickup lines to The Makeup Misses. While slapping fives as the three females found space onboard Bobby's pickup, the driver ignored Fish, who showed he was impressed by yelling out his name throughout their slow exit off school grounds. They were a cocky crew of seniors whose leader was too cool to care about underclassmen who assumed they could compete. Bobby's father, The Barrel, owned Venoa Beach Gun & Pawn near the rail on the state road and often went hunting with Mayor Mark, who bought school lunch as often as they traded guns. Bobby and The Bang Busters borrowed rifles out the showcase in the shop to shoot bears in the open on the barren road. As

Bobby drove away, Blake told his own crew of friends that they were better with more bass than them, even with no name.

"Besides, Bobby's a brat," he said.

"At least he can afford to soup up his ride working for his dad. Man, I'm tired of mowing lawns," complained Big Ant.

"They all work there and helped him," Blake told him, "Just like we helped Fish pay for the deck, amps, and the subs."

"Business is booming for The Barrel more than the bass is in Fish's trunk!" assumed Haywood.

"Yea, no girls are in my backseat," said Fish.

Blake grabbed him by the hair and said, "Because they wouldn't fit with us in it!"

"Watch the curls," he said, as Messy Molly from Venoa Park approached them with her sneakers untied.

"Hey, fishy poo," she said, lifting her skirt, "isn't my tattoo amazing?"

"It's cool, when did you get it?"

"Yesterday from Rosemary! She's so amazing," she said, and kissed him on the nose.

Rosemary's Tattoo Parlor between the fine graffiti walls of Venoa Beach Mall was where Messy Molly forged her mother's consent. She paid with a balled-up bunch of bills she saved from recycling and a new pair of roller skates.

Rosemary wore out her old ones skating around the mall pitching her parlor as The Scooter Crew rode by after slapping fives with Supervisor Sam.

While Messy Molly played in Fish's hair, Haywood asked her, "Are you going to Jessica's party?"

"Nope," said the blond.

"Why not?" asked Fish.

"Because The Scooter Crew's doing donuts at the rail!"

Part 3: Jessica

"Wow, Jess's parents are the coolest!" a male exclaimed, running around shirtless with an empty cup. Teenagers from every neighborhood in town attended from Venoa Lakes to Venoa Crossing near the paved trail. They threw napkins on the floor and left stains on the walls from spilled punch. Few raced up and down the carpet stairs stepping over Jessica and her close friends who sat admiring the senior studs standing in the foyer. As two other males with muscle hopped over furniture, chasing girls out the backdoor into the pool, she made her way through the dancing crowd to the front door for air.

"Hey, Jessica," said Haywood, avoiding Mandy who was over admiring him after beating her in a cursing contest.

"Hey," she tied her braids in a ponytail, "it's warm out here."

"Like my heart is for the hunnies," he said.

"Really?" and she beamed with her brown eyes wide before asking, "Do you know what girls at school say about you?"

"No, what?"

"They say that they know there's something special about them when Hero goes out of his way to say hello," as another shirtless male ran through the open garage. Two girls in bikini tops chased him with hot water guns while screaming their threats to others on the lawn.

"So, then there's something special about you."

As next year's senior head cheerleader, she boasted, "Well, I am really popular," she got serious, "but not as much as Bobby is with the girls."

"You want to date Bobby? I didn't know you liked white guys."

"Bobby and I were almost a real couple until Patty moved into his neighborhood," she confided to him.

Pretty Patty was pale as the palms of Lady of Red's hands and wore heels that made a sound in the hall that no male at Venoa Beach High could ignore. She was a brunette with glossed lips and a wink that made boys like Bobby want to be men. While in school, Pretty Patty, Jesse, and their other friends who remained at the party would trade clothes they bought with credit cards they applied for in their mothers' name. Pretty Patty believed that to look good was to distract the pride of boys, causing them to compromise.

"Is she here?"

"She's with him at the rail."

"When I see him at graduation, I'm going to give him a piece of my mind," fumed Haywood, and he called over his three friends who were sharing a cigarette on the lawn. Jessica refused a smoke from Fish who stole a pack from Aunt Kate who was avoiding the IRS and sleeping at his house.

"What did she do?" asked Jessica.

"Tax fraud or something like that," said Fish.

"Really? Well, that's what to expect from a Venoan, isn't it?"

With a yo-yo on each hand and a girl in pajamas on his arm, Big Ant asked Haywood, "So, why did you call us over here, man?"

"Bobby ditched her for Pretty Patty, and you know how we feel about the ladies," he said, and Blake put his arm around Jessica. He told her that Bobby was not good for her before asking her to hook him up with one of her friends inside. He held the front door open before the two of them walked through the dancing crowd in the living room to the backdoor. When they noticed her friends lazing by the pool, Blake checked his breath, filled his mouth with gum like Fish does, and cracked his neck before following her out the door.

Part 4: Grandpa?

A shirtless Blake jumped into the pool holding hands with Becca who was wearing a bra and begging Jessica to join them. Becca splashed her when she refused before Blake put Jessica's friend on his shoulders and water walked until she fell underneath. She was still catching her breath when he picked her up by her thighs and carried her across the pool to the diving board. With her legs wrapped around his waist, they made out as Man appeared through the window locking arms with Lady of Red.

"There's an old couple in the kitchen!" blurted a freckled female as she ran out the backdoor in filthy overalls from a food fight before the old folks' arrival.

Jessica looked and thought, "Grandpa?" and she went inside, following behind others who were also curious.

"Who's the old man?" someone asked her, as the teenagers surrounded them as the two fed each other tortilla chips after dipping them in cheese. Some of it fell on the orthopedic shoes Man wore with a tailored suit and tie that matched the headpiece his date was wearing. Lady of Red stood in red heels and a sparkling gown that made the teenage boys adjust their posture. Jessica admired her beauty before tapping Man on the shoulder. He was sniffing her neck aroused by her perfume.

"Excuse me, sir, but I don't think you're at the right place." she said.

"Well, hello, young lady. Would you like some dip?"

"I think she wants to know what we're doing here," said Lady of Red, scooping herself some punch.

"Well, we're here to party!"

"But how did you even know about my party?"

He smiled and said, "The Bass Boys. Pardon us while we find space on the dance floor," and she stood puzzled as the old began to dance among the young. When Haywood and Big Ant appeared in the crowd with Fish behind them twirling, Jessica waved her hands for their attention.

The three of them surrounded her when she asked, "Who are The Bass Boys?"

"Man, I don't know," said Big Ant, and he looked off into the dancing crowd, "but I know that's the old guy from our neighborhood."

"You guys know him?"

"We let him in," said Haywood.

She said, "Really?" and threw her hairband on the floor. She shook her braids and complained, "Now, who's going to come to my party next year thinking that I invited an old man to my last one?"

"He was with Lady of Red," explained Big Ant. "Man, would you look at her?"

"She's beautiful," said Haywood.

"Gorgeous," said Fish.

Jessica thought out loud, "So, then you guys must be The Bass Boys he was talking about. Fish, where are those invites I gave you?"

"Well, what happened was," he scratched his chin, "I was speeding in circles around the neighborhood while we were listening to music, and they just kinda flew out."

"He must have found one," said Haywood.

"But why would he come to a teenage girl's party?" she asked.

"Because he's a Venoan? I don't know, man," said Big Ant, as Blake came inside with his arm around Becca who was beaming with pride. As they made their way to where Jessica stood with the other three boys, he noticed his old neighbors as they sat on the sofa massaging each other's shoulders. Man closed his eyes as Lady of Red rubbed him careful not to break her nails. While it was her turn, she moaned like she was in love with him and begged him not to stop. The teenagers continued to party around them as if they were as young as sprouting freshman. Someone even brought them drinks to cool off before asking them to join them in a game of cards.

As they sat at the kitchen table to play, Blake approached them, rapping with Becca on his back and said, "Nice clothes."

"Well, thank you," said Man, "a lovely lady should make every man want to look their best."

"And a gentleman should make a lady want to do the same," said Lady of Red, counting her cards.

"This is the other Bass Boy I was telling you about."

"Handsome," she said, and Blake introduced them to his new friend who they welcomed to the neighborhood assuming she would be visiting. Becca blushed as Lady of Red complimented her highlighted hair and painted toenails before whispering something in her ear.

"Girl talk?" asked Blake, before a commotion outside caught their attention.

Jessica checked her makeup and then yanked Becca by the arm and said, "Oh my gosh, Bobby's here."

Part 5: Bobby

Some from the dancing crowd scattered outside. Bobby revved the engine while The Bang Busters were howling in the cargo bed with open longnecks. The sound of the exhaust awoke some neighbors who stood on their lawns with their phones recording Bobby on camera as he showed off his ride. When The Bang Busters jumped out the back, he followed behind them sipping liquor from a flask with Pretty Patty holding his free hand. He wasted the rest on the road before walking up Jessica's driveway where she stood in the open garage with Becca and the four boys.

"Well, what's up, Jess?" he said.

"Don't say anything to him," Blake told her, as she stood with her arms folded.

"She has already told me everything I wanted to hear and more," Bobby said, and slapped fives with his followers who howled at the moon.

"How was I?" asked Jessica.

"I have to admit it was as good as you look."

Haywood stepped closer to him and said, "I hope you came here to apologize, you punk."

The Bang Busters laughed, and one said, "Looks like someone's ready to fight."

Haywood spat.

"Look, he's balling up his fists," said the other, while Bobby was kissing Pretty Patty.

"Now, tell her you're sorry," she said.

"Okay," said Bobby, wiping the gloss from his lips. "Jess, I'm sorry for thinking that you can make me feel the way she can."

Haywood punched him.

Bobby massaged his jaw and tasted his own blood before telling Haywood, "You can punch, but can you fight?"

Pretty Patty was pleading with him to take her home when Jessica warned Haywood, "He's too strong!"

After throwing the first punch and tripping over his own feet, Haywood grabbed him by the knee in attempt to stand. Bobby kicked him to the concrete and then picked him up by his chin. He punched him in the face and laughed as Haywood fell flat on his back. The senior was hovered over the sophomore, pounding him to a pulp when Big Ant rushed to his aid. When The Bang Busters intervened, Blake threw his own pair of punches. Fish spit his gum out and jumped on one's back, trying to choke him. The older teenagers tussled with the underclassmen as Man stepped outside the front door with his shoes off.

"Ah," he smiled, "there you boys are," while the gallant four gathered to regroup.

"You see this right here, old man," said Bobby, pulling Pretty Patty close, "only a man can manage a woman like this."

"Woman?" said Lady of Red, stepping out the shadows. Bobby and The Bang Busters stood wide eyed as Man took her by the hand and kissed it. She stood behind him after she was asked if she would allow him to address the arrogant athlete whose athletic prowess was assumed by his stature.

"Let me ask him," he whispered to her, and he turned to Bobby and said, "Do you play sports, son?"

"I'm a four-time wrestling champion," said Bobby, and he and The Bang Busters howled.

"You know, I used to play basketball in my youth, but the taller my teammates got, the shorter I became, though I am taller than average men."

He looked at Pretty Patty and said, "Yea, well, wrestling's a man's sport, right babe?" Patty assured him with a smile.

Man laughed and then got serious to say, "Son, the value of a man is measured by the size of his heart, not his muscle or loins," and he looked him in the eyes. Bobby and The Bang Busters walked back to his pickup with their heads low.

"Wait, boys," said the star athlete, "I want to invite the old man to my graduation cookout," and he walked up to him and swung his fist. Man dodged the blow and swept the senior's feet.

Bobby was stumbling back to his pickup when Haywood asked, "You know karate?"

"Sure I do, young man," he said, "and you know what else I love?"

"What?" they asked.

"Music like The Bass Boys do."

The four boys thought, "The Bass Boys, that *is* us."

"So, I want you boys to come by my store downtown," he said, "where I have some old records with bass that will leave your ears ringing for days."

Part 6: The Bass Boys

The Bass Boys were at separate posts communicating through two-way radios as the seniors walked single file to their seats. Big Ant surveyed the parking lot while Blake stood inside by the doors. Haywood sat at the top of the bleachers with a brunette from the party as Messy Molly played in Fish's hair on the bottom row.

"And you know what else was amazing?"

"No, what?" Fish replied.

"The Scooter Crew's practice show at the skate park. Right after their show at the rail, Scott who lives in my neighborhood invited me himself!"

"I've seen them after school, but how many different kinds of scooters do they know how to ride?"

"All kinds!"

As Principal Jon took to the podium, Fish answered the roger beep from Blake and confirmed, "We're still waiting until the recession starts, right?"

"Affirmative," said Blake.

"Bobby's sitting right in the middle," said Haywood. "There's no way he's getting up before they call his row, over."

"So, we should do it now?"

"Man, copy that."

"Wait," said Fish, "I'm looking straight at The Bang Busters, and if I can see them, then they can see me."

"So, then don't get up," said Blake, "and Haywood you stay there to keep an eye on Bobby."

"Man, I'm ready when you are, Blake," and the two met outside at Fish's car to further their plan.

Big Ant opened the trunk and tossed Blake a bag of ice picks and awls. They put on face shields after Big Ant pocketed a sharp knife and hammer and eased their way to Bobby's pickup with nails in their teeth. As Blake began slashing the tires on one side, Big Ant banged nails into the ones on the other. When one ice pick or awl became dull, Blake used another still with nails in his teeth. He made a hole when Big Ant passed him the hammer to ensure the tires deflate before graduation was over. The yo-yoing Bass Boy pulled out the knife, felt the edge, and stabbed the tire until it made a loud noise. When they finished removing the nails, the two Bass Boys crept back to the car to stash the supplies before walking inside the building.

"Blake, what's your location?" Fish asked over the radio.

"We're back in," he said.

"Well, how did it go?"

"Man, piece of cake."

"There's room for you guys up here, over," and they stepped up the bleachers through the crowd as the recession continued. The brunette shouted for Principal Jon as he left the stage. Bobby looked up to see as he slapped fives with The Bang Busters while breaking formation.

"Hey, man, do you think he saw us?"

"The plan was to do damage control anyway," said Haywood.

"Relax, guys," said Blake, "we're Venoans, remember?" and they received a roger beep from Fish as few folks were making their way to the exit.

He said, "I just saw The Barrel, and he's heading Bobby's way. Do you copy?"

"Man, copy that," and they met Fish at the door.

"Alright, guys, remember we're acting," said Blake, as more people left their place in the bleachers to praise the graduates gathered on the gymnasium floor. Bobby and The Bang Busters stood with his father when The Bass Boys started to pretend.

"Hey, Bobbo," said Fish, "looking good in that cap and gown."

"Yea, man, congratulations!"

"We just wanted to come here to apologize for what happened at Jessica's party," said Blake.

"Yea," said Haywood, "what was I thinking trying to go up against you."

"That old man was lucky," said Fish, and Bobby nodded.

"Well, enjoy yourself at the cookout, man."

"Save us a plate, we might come by," said Haywood.

"Uh, I don't like potato salad," said Fish, "so you can substitute it with macaroni and cheese, maybe?"

"No ice cream, though," said Blake, "because Hero over here is lactose intolerant."

"Well, later, you guys," and Bobby and The Bang Busters squinted at them as they walked away. The five sophomores including Messy Molly stood outside by Fish's car waiting for Bobby and The Bang Busters to appear in the parking lot. As the brunette shouted her goodbyes to Haywood, Big Ant rushed to Bobby's pickup to check the tires. He was picking up leftover nails when The Bang Busters saw him and called for Bobby who was babbling with the babes.

"Anthony, let's go!" yelled Blake, as the senior crew scurried across the parking lot. With Messy Molly squished between Blake and Haywood in the backseat, Fish pulled out the parking space and pushed the passenger side door open. As Big Ant ran to the car, Bobby hopped in his pickup and revved the engine with The Bang Busters in the back. The Bass Boys laughed out the car windows as the truck jerked through the parking lot. With Big Ant safe in the front seat, Fish turned up the music always with the bass above treble and drove away.

Part 7: Music

Man was taking down signs outside his store when the boys drove up yelling, "We got him!" with their heads out the windows.

"Ah, The Bass Boys," he said, "I knew you would come."

"You should've seen it!" said Haywood, as they hopped out.

"Yea," said Fish, "it could barely move."

"They almost caught us, man."

"But we did it exactly how you showed us," said Blake.

Man stood silent.

"What's wrong?" asked Haywood.

"I believe that I told you boys the wrong thing to do," said Man, and they looked confused. "Have The Bass Boys ever heard the story of The Homicidal Homeowner?"

With his arm around Messy Molly, Fish said, "No, tell us."

"I promise to tell you boys the tale after you all have taken your own tour, so come on in," and they followed him inside.

When he turned on the lights, there were wall posters, old ticket stubs in frames, karate trophies, instruments mounted on the ceiling above the stage floor, and a wide selection of music from the sales floor down the aisles.

"Were you a singer?" asked Haywood.

Man said, "No, I was a drummer," and smiled. "Go on, take a look around," and they scattered.

Fish chased Messy Molly to a quiet spot in the aisle where they kissed as Big Ant was sampling reggae music in a pair of headphones. Blake read magazines while Haywood browsed CDs. While it was quiet, Man turned on some house music, pulled out his drumsticks, and began beating the counter like it was a snare.

"You're amazing!"

"Where did you learn how to play like that?" asked Fish.

Still going, he said, "Preacher Paul's church. He conceived a child with my daughter and stayed with his wife. I told him to give me the drum set or else I'll put my knee to his skull. Would you like to see it?"

"Yea," they said, and Fish called for his three friends to meet them in the back. Big Ant was unable to hear with headphones on and realized he was alone after opening his eyes when the song ended. He went to where Man sat at his drum set surrounded by the other Bass Boys and howled like Bobby and The Bang Busters did.

"Sounds better when you do it," said Blake, as Man was beating the tom-tom and the symbols. He switched to the snare before adding the bass drum and they danced. After surrounding Fish as he showed off his moves, The Bass Boys, with Messy Molly in the middle, followed Man to the front as he carried a case of vinyl records to the counter.

"Whoa, hip hop," the boys said, as they pulled from the case.

"Old school," he said.

"Do these records still work?" asked Haywood.

"They sure do."

"There's the record player," said Blake, pointing. "Pass me one," and he ran over to spin it.

"Turn it up, man," and they danced when he did. Fish was twirling Messy Molly on her toes when the record started to scratch and was begging to fix it.

Man smiled and said, "Nope, because it's time for another order of business," and he reached in his pocket for a set of keys and tossed it to Blake.

He caught it and asked, "What are these for?"

"They're the keys to the store."

"You want us to work here?" asked Haywood.

"I want you boys run it like it's yours."

"Sounds good, but why?" asked Blake.

"Well, I'm old," he said, "and my daughter Pickney doesn't want me to."

"Well, I'm in," said Fish.

"Me too," said Haywood.

"I got your back, music man," said Big Ant.

Messy Molly gave Man a flower from his own vase on the counter when Blake pocketed the keys and said, "We all do," and Man passed him another record to spin, and they danced.

Part 8: Flowers

Man stood outside Lady of Red's home with a large bouquet of roses and The Bass Boys in his shadow holding one small arrangement of flowers each. They were all in ties and talking among themselves when she appeared at the window in a red robe with her hair curled, wearing glasses at the tip of her nose. The boys saw her and tightened their ties as she came to the door carrying a book.

She opened it before Man said, "I hope we're not disturbing you."

"I was at the climax," she said.

"So, then we should come back another time."

"With all those flowers?"

"They're for you," said Haywood, and handed her his set.

"You see, lovely," he gave her the bouquet, "the boys wanted to come with me to thank you for attending the party with me. Without you, I would've made a weak impression on the boys causing them to disagree to run my store."

She smelled the roses and said, "Flowers are as dear to my heart as a gentleman who calls me lovely," so the boys all called her lovely before she invited them in for tea.

There were flowers from the foyer to the living room and into the kitchen where The Bass Boys sat practicing their new handshake. Some were in vases, some were in tubs, some were plastic, and others were painted on canvases. While complimenting her decor, Man assisted Lady of Red as she prepared their cups singing to her new flowers below her breath. She poured their tea standing on a rug the shape of a garden flower and asked him if he noticed the sofa was yellow like the petals of sunflowers. Man replied with a smile and sipped his tea as she brought the boys theirs on a tray.

"Now, you don't drink it," she told them. "You sip it," and they did.

"Didn't you pretend to be Ms. Lily?" asked Fish.

"Yes," said Lady of Red.

Haywood asked, "Can you tell us the story?"

"Well, I'm not ashamed of it. I'm a Venoan," she said, "and I should tell you gentlemen, so you understand what it means to be one," and Man pulled her a chair.

Lady of Red crossed her legs causing the boys to stretch their necks for a glimpse at her thighs as she began the story. She told them she and Lily met as members of Venoa Beach High's volleyball team and became friends. Lily lived in Venoa Oaks with her parents, who she killed by hiding their medication.

Blake asked, "Why did she do it?"

"For life insurance."

"What did she buy?"

"A glasshouse, which made me jealous," she admitted.

Lady of Red visited Lily for a day of gardening when she crept upstairs and rubbed poison oak on her pillow. Before heading downstairs, she stole a wig and a pair of overalls from the closet before snatching the key to the greenhouse off the dresser. She made a copy of the key at Venoa Beach Drug Store off the state road and planted it in Lily's car. Lady of Red called her every day waiting for her to tell her she was ill. When she admitted her skin was bright red from scratching, Lady of Red furthered her plan.

"What did you do?" asked Haywood.

"So, I put on her overalls, styled the wig like she does, and sat for days ordering exotic seeds to grow in my garden."

Preacher Paul's wife First Lady came by to pick fruit, Catherine the librarian showed up for her fair share, and even Gwen from the neighborhood assumed she was Lily. When Sheriff Shawn appeared looking for his vegetables Lily always set aside for him, he noticed a strand of red hair hanging as she was picking ones she assumed he liked. He asked her where Lily was before allowing her to go free after they shared a good laugh.

Fish said, "You're bold."

"Also brave like all Venoans who don't fear consequences."

"Fearless, man."

"And we don't take ourselves too seriously," as she uncrossed her legs to cross them again.

Man said, "When I was in Venoa Beach Juvenile Jail for selling false identification cards, it was humility that got me through as well as others."

"But we learn as Venoans that wrong is to be done for the good. Plants give off oxygen, allowing us to breath."

Fish said, "Molly's my oxygen. We're not together, but I think she knows it."

"Women worthwhile are like flowers," she said, "needing light to grow their colors for the world to see. That's why you won't find us at nightclubs where it's dark inside."

"Are you going to come by when we open? I promise the lights will be on," said Blake.

Part 9: Open

"Thank you for shopping at The Music Man," said Blake, after cashing out a customer. While Fish played with Big Ant's yo-yo conscious of customers carrying copies of CDs without having sampled the songs first, Haywood slept in the backseat of the car outside. Big Ant sat at the second cash register preparing to place an order as a line was forming at the counter. More came in when Fish yelled out his name to put the pen down. Blake's line got shorter as he ignored the passes from young women, sending them over to Big Ant who began pitching the store's new online streaming service to limit the cash count at closing.

"Hey, man, can you break a fifty?"

"Let me check," said Blake, as Fish was two-stepping to encourage customers to buy.

Meanwhile, Haywood was standing outside the car smoking and tired from running the register. When Bobby and The Bang Busters drove by in a rental, he put out his cigarette unaware of the graduated group, who saw him as he was walking towards the store and hopped out.

Bobby exclaimed, "Come here, boy!" before grabbing him by his collar. "So, you and your friends thought it was funny slashing my tires."

"Kill me," said Haywood.

The Bang Busters noticed the rest of The Bass Boys inside when one said, "There they are."

Bobby said, "So, this is where the boys hang out?"

"We work for the old man."

"Yea, well, here's another lesson for you," he said. "Keep your eyes open," and they walked away.

Haywood walked inside when Big Ant yelled, "Man, you know the music man still hasn't told us The Homicidal Homeowner story?"

Part 10: Bang

Bobby aimed at the bullseye in his backyard while The Bang Busters loaded rifles on the back porch. When he hit the center after unloading a few shots, he switched guns and aimed at the dummy on a tree before pulling the trigger.

"That's good shooting, Bobby," said The Barrel, as he drank whiskey standing behind him with a shotgun in is free hand. Bobby reloaded and pulled the trigger a few times before The Barrel aimed and destroyed it with two rounds.

"You could've let me finish," Bobby told his father.

"You weren't going to get it like that with that weapon." He wiped the barrel and said, "This is a man's gun."

"I thought every gun was a man's gun."

"Yea, well, this one is a real man's gun," said The Barrel.

Bobby dropped his weapon on the grass and yelled out to The Bang Busters, "Hey, boys, let's take a ride!" as The Barrel practiced his aim.

Bobby and The Bang Busters parked outside Venoa Beach Pawn before Bobby unlocked the showcase inside. He put the rifles back and took shotguns tossing them to the two. They looked confused as Bobby put on gloves to load his weapon and asked him if they were going to the barren road.

"No," he said, before driving them downtown with him.

"That's the old man from the party," said one of The Bang Busters, as Man walked in behind Haywood who was outside smoking.

Bobby parked and said, "Come on, boys."

"We're not going to kill anybody, are we?" asked the other one.

Bobby snapped, "Both of you stay here!" and covered the shotgun with a towel and walked towards the store.

Meanwhile, The Bass Boys stood surrounding Man as he began telling the story of The Homicidal Homeowner.

"He lived in Venoa Gardens," he said, as the doors swung open.

"Uh, we're not open today," said Fish.

Bobby pointed the shotgun and said, "That's alright because I've got all the heavy metal I need."

"You're going to kill us for slashing your tires?" asked Blake.

"No, I'm going to kill him for trying to be the kind of father to me that I never had," and he yelled, "Bang!" pulling the trigger.

"Call the cops!" as Bobby walked out.

"No," said Man, collapsing, "let him go."

Haywood said, "Bobby warned me."

"He warned you, and you didn't tell us?" asked Fish.

"Calm down," said Blake.

"No, we could've prepared!"

"Prepared for what, man? We wouldn't have known what he was going to do!"

"Venoans don't fear consequences," said Blake.

With tears flowing, Fish stood over Man and said, "You never finished telling us the story."

"He killed with kindness," he said and died.

Story 2
Neighbors Of
Venoa Gardens

Part 1: Out

The Mowing Man was bathing in the fountain when Neglected Nikki appeared and said, "You know my mom would've let you shower at our place, right?"

"Kicked out again, huh?"

"Her boyfriend's over who looks damn near my age," she sat barefoot on the grass. "She wants to make it seem as if she doesn't have any kids whenever he's around."

"She wants to feel like an ol' teenager," said The Mowing Man, drying his chest with his shirt.

Neglected Nikki laughed and said, "She thinks I should go back to Venoa Beach High to wait until my senior year to find a freshman boyfriend I can control."

"Having the ol' upper hand is what they call it," he said, "but in real love, no one has an upper hand," and walked away pushing his lawnmower with his boots untied.

Neglected Nikki sat there picking at the grass while people drove by honking their horns at her new haircut. She dipped her hands in the water and wet her bangs before starting down the sidewalk. She was a blond who became brunette after losing a bet between her and Will as two out of the three members of The Dropouts. With Graves as the third and thorough thinker, Neglected Nikki was always in the middle of rifts between the two boys as they argued about who would lead their projects. They were a creative crew of caring cohorts with constant ideas they assumed would afford their way out of Venoa Beach and into a villa in Major City.

"Want to hang out?" Neglected Nikki asked Will after knocking on his window.

He laughed and said, "Nice haircut."

"Then, what's so funny?"

He shrugged his shoulders and said, "Hey, now that's it's black, are you having any dark thoughts?" sticking his head further out the window and smiling.

"I am actually," said Neglected Nikki, "so let me in, so I can kill you for making me bet on a baseball game that I know nothing about!"

"You wouldn't hurt a fly," he said.

"Just let me in," and she climbed through the window.

There were clothes on the floor covering tools and balled up blueprints on his desk and dresser where his trophies were aligned in a row. Neglected Nikki slid off her flip-flops and stepped on a nail before finding space on his bed to treat her wound.

After getting a first aid kit, Will said, "Now, stay still," applying ointment.

She turned on the news and asked, "Did you hear about what happened?"

"No, turn it up."

The anchorman reported, "A man was shot and killed in his store in Downtown Venoa Beach. In route of its reopening, there were no cameras installed inside or outside of the establishment. The four teenage boys who work there found his body but were unable to provide police any leads. Chief Earl has begun an investigation that will continue until justice is served."

"Do you think the boys set him up?"

"Nah," said Will.

She joked, "Maybe The Homicidal Homeowner is back for more revenge!"

"He didn't use tangible weapons, remember? Anyways, that story's not even true."

"Venoans don't fear consequences, so it could be anybody," she said.

"That's why we got to get out of Venoa!" exclaimed Will.

"Got any new ideas?"

He threw a baseball at his closet door and yelled, "I'm all out of ideas!" and then his phone rang.

"It's Graves," she said and answered it before Will drove himself crazy.

Part 2: Crazy?

Graves rushed over from work at Venoa Beach Service Station off the state road to where Will was with Neglected Nikki rattling his brain. When he walked in, the dropout who once drug his foot at the mound was banging his desk with a baseball bat trying to come up with something to create.

"We're never. Going. To get. Out of here," he said and threw the bat down.

"Easy there, killer, relax," said Graves, greasing his hair with the product he always kept in his pocket.

Neglected Nikki joked, "He's on his cycle."

"This is serious," asserted Will. "A matter of life and death," and he sat in his chair with his elbows on his knees. As Neglected Nikki was twirling his hanging braids to calm him, Graves pulled out his phone to record them on camera.

"What are you doing, Graves?" she asked.

"I want him to remember this," he said, getting a closeup, "because it's the last time he'll ever feel this way after we're done killing it."

"Done killing what?"

"Putting together my new killer idea that I promise is going to make all our dreams come true," said Graves, "so frown for the camera," and Will put his shirt over his head.

"How did you come up with it?" she asked, and he told her to sit before beginning the story.

He was getting ready for work when he misplaced his phone after a brief conversation with his next-door neighbor Mandy, who cursed out the student body in her speech during the school election and spent her detention playing chess with Principal Jon. Graves ended the call and tossed it after Mandy demanded more dollars for babysitting his brother Davey and dodged his advances with her hostile disposition. Minutes before he was supposed to clock in, he found it on the floor by the fridge with mean texts from Mandy. Graves replied with a smiley face and rushed to work before losing it again. After searching the entire service station, between cashing out customers, he found it on top of his car with a voice message from Mandy cursing him out.

Neglected Nikki said, "You didn't deserve that."

"Wait, I'm not done," he said. "The next part kills," and he told them that a man pushing a cotton candy machine parked it next to him when he pondered.

"And?" she said.

"That's when I came up with The Crazy Cupid Machine," he boasted.

The two thought, "Crazy?"

"What does it do?" asked Will.

"It makes your crush have a crush on you."

Part 3: Crush

Greta parked in her driveway with her husband Gary in the front seat. They were bookmakers whose winnings funded the library services downtown. She stepped out the car to smell the pine in the air before opening the passenger side door for Gary, who walked with a cane to the front door as she stood soaking in the sun. She was Black as her square toe heels and walked with a waddle through the garage into their home.

"I held the door open for you, sweetheart," said Gary, sitting in his favorite chair.

"Oh, I must not have been paying any attention," she said.

"You weren't paying any more attention to me than I was to Preacher Paul."

From the kitchen, she raised her voice and said, "Well, at least his eulogy was a lot shorter than his sermons."

"Do you still wish you could've married the deceased?"

"Oh, yes," said Greta, bringing Gary some water, "my first crush was on Man," and she sat on the sofa to reread the obituary before the doorbell rang.

"Who is it?!" asked Gary, as Greta was going to see.

She opened the door and said, "Chile, don't tell me she kicked you out, again."

Neglected Nikki smiled saying, "Hey, Mrs. Greta, any dumplings?"

"I'm always surprised by how much you can eat as small as your waist is," she said. "C'mon in, chile, so I can feed you because God knows what your mama got in her fridge. Too busy crushing on those younger men while your own daughter's starving to death."

"Is that Nicole?" asked Gary from the living room.

"Yea, it's her," said Greta, preparing leftovers while Neglected Nikki sat at the kitchen table with her feet in the chair.

"Can you give me extra? I want to save some for The Mowing Man," she said.

Greta revealed The Mowing Man had a serious crush on Woman Supreme who lived on the cul-de-sac. While at the funeral, Greta was among others in a circle around Woman Supreme as she told them her story about the man who roams Venoa Gardens without a house to call home. He caught her at the mailbox, still in her heels after work, and offered to cut her grass for free. After he was finished, she let him shower before he offered to cook for her.

"What does she do?" asked Neglected Nikki with a mouthful.

"Chile, she's secretary to Mayor Mark."

Gary raised his voice asking, "Do you remember when she passed out wine glasses at the rally and got everyone wasted?"

"Oh, yes," laughed Greta before finishing the story.

She said Woman Supreme and The Mowing Man sat in silence and ate with her son Lincoln at their feet. Before leaving, he washed the dishes and left a note for her on a napkin.

"What did it say?"

"Love," she said, and she poured her more water.

"That's sweet," said Neglected Nikki.

"Chile, he has left her that same note in her mailbox ever since."

Gary walked in and joked, "Nicole ate all our food again, huh? And the weight goes straight to her thighs," and he sat down beside her while Greta heated up his food.

"Having a crush can drive you crazy like a good meal can put your mind at ease," said Greta.

"You know, I have a crush, too, Mrs. Greta."

"Chile, on who?"

"My friend Will, he's Black."

Part 4: Black

People parked their cars in a line outside the gate, waiting for their children to return from summer school with progress reports to sign. Some walked from their homes to stand to await the students, and among them was Will. With an open magazine, he stood beside Craig, nicknamed "Gentleman" for his politeness. The white man who stole a dead man's identity to open a gentleman's club in Major City that ran as a study hall during the day always wore black. He believed it gave him power over people who preyed on the proud like himself. He lived in a house with a two-car garage and was handing out fliers for his next neighborhood sale. Will took one and slid it between the pages before the bus drove up to unload the boisterous boys and girls.

"Dave, over here!" exclaimed Will.

Davey ran yelling, "Will!" and jumped into his arms.

"How was school, little man?"

"I drew a bear and colored him black," he said.

"Heard about the barren road one too many times, huh?"

"Graves says he's going to take me there, but I want to keep one as a pet, so I can make it eat people."

"I guess that's kind of the way Venoans think," said Will, standing him up on the sidewalk.

As Gentleman Craig walked away with his daughter, he shouted, "Are you guys going to come by this weekend?"

"Yea," replied Will, "we've started a new project and need parts, so we'll be there!"

Davey tapped him and asked, "Are you taking me to Mandy's house?"

"Nah, since school's out, she got a job at the mall to enjoy her time off without having to be bothered babysitting little boys like you," he said.

"Why do I have to go to school in the summer?"

"So, you don't end up like The Dropouts," and he opened the front door to find his uncle arranging artwork that he bribed for with blank checks to a closed account, "Hey, go in my room and do your homework," Will told Davey. "What do you have there, Uncle Moe?"

"Portraits of Black people," he said and showed him. "It's important that people who enter our home feel free to express themselves like artists do so courageously."

"None of them are smiling."

"Because experience taught them to protect themselves. Black is a symbol of protection," and he hung one over the sofa.

"Well, my friends are white," said Will, staring at the picture, "and we protect each other."

"Black also symbolizes elegance and sophistication," said Uncle Moe, hanging another.

"Doesn't it also symbolize death?"

Part 5: Mourning

Beyond the broken fence that guarded the backyards of houses closest to it from critters and deer that roamed the woods was where The Mowing Man sat singing in his shed. With tears flowing, he stared at a taped photograph hanging from a nail and reminisced as the words from the song resonated. The Mowing Man would bang the back of his head on the shed when memories were too fond compared to his current life. When critters came, he sang louder, assuming they could understand because he wanted someone to relate.

He heard voices when he asked one, "Who's that, ol' muskrat?" and grabbed some binoculars to see. "Is it her, back from the dead?" Graves appeared with Neglected Nikki.

"There he is," he said.

"Hey, we brought you some dinner, hungry?"

The Mowing Man started to sing.

"Do you have any parts we could use?"

Neglected Nikki walked closer to him and said, "That's a nice song."

"A nice ol' song for a nice woman," he said, and kept singing.

"Is that her in the picture?"

"Yup," and he wiped his tears.

They were sitting in the shed when Graves asked, "Did she get killed?"

"Yup."

"How?"

"*Fire*," said The Mowing Man, and began telling his story.

He ran a landscaping business that his wife Elanor helped him build with money from her office job in Major City. The Mowing Man admitted she was the breadwinner for a while before his business was established.

"Some people get married for financial security, others pick a person that can help them fulfill what they believe their purpose to be, and few do it for love."

"Why did you get married?" asked Neglected Nikki.

"Ol' security," he admitted, "though she did it for love."

Elanor and The Mowing Man moved from Venoa Crossing to Venoa Gardens after she received a promotion that guaranteed her time off. The dresser covered with burning candles caught fire that spread throughout their bedroom as they slept after she surprised him with sex. He tried to carry Elanor to safety as she snored but was too weak.

Graves said, "The fumes killed her first."

"I lost the house, my business, my wife, and a life I would kill ol' Mayor Mark to have back."

"But you still have memories," said Neglected Nikki.

"And my ol' equipment, especially this one here," he said, spinning the wheels on his lawnmower.

"Speaking of killer equipment, do you have anything you don't use anymore? We need some parts."

"I kind of want to keep all my ol' stuff."

Neglected Nikki rushed to stand, "Hey, maybe we can help you! I know you've got a crush on Woman Supreme."

"Yea!" exclaimed Graves. "If you give us some of your stuff to take apart, we can guarantee you'll get your life back, at least love!" and he did after singing Elanor's favorite song.

Part 6: Parts

People stood in Gentleman Craig's driveway as the garage doors opened.

He echoed through a bullhorn, "Grab an item, please, grab your wallet, please, and grab my attention, please!"

There was a radio, television with a remote, computer monitor with a keyboard, CD player, toaster, and microwave, among other devices. Some neighbors surrounded the grandfather clock placing their bids. Few dug their hands in the bins full of books and toys. Others tried on clothes and shoes while sitting in the lounge chairs for sale.

"Oh, I love this dress!" exclaimed Neglected Nikki.

"We're here for parts," said Will.

"We already got some of the basic components."

"So, what do we need?"

Graves said, "Nikki's got the list."

"I thought you had it," she said.

"Forget the list," said Will. "Grab all the electronics." The Mowing Man appeared and stared into his eyes. "Uh, hello, sir."

"Yea, thanks for the parts!"

Neglected Nikki asked him, "Are you okay?" and he smiled hiding his teeth before walking away.

As they were filling their bags with items off the tables, Will asked, "What was that all about?"

"What do you mean?" asked Graves. "He likes us. He's a killer singer," and they stood in line to pay as Mandy walked up the driveway turning everyone's attention to her mood. With her hair straightened pass her shoulders in a sundress and sandals, she twirled her gum around her finger and pushed people out her way with her free hand.

"That's who you have a crush on?" asked Neglected Nikki.

"She's sexy," said Graves.

"But she's mean."

Someone yelled, "Hey, Gentleman, where did you get this electric scooter?"

He replied, "My nephew Scott is part of some group called The Scooter Crew and wanted me to test it out!"

Part 7: Test

Uncle Moe admired the artwork in the living room with a guitar while The Dropouts boasted in Will's bedroom. With screws on the floor and nuts and bolts scattered on the furniture, The Crazy Cupid Machine stood shining on the throw rug. The two boys took care of the building while Neglected Nikki color coordinated the exterior. They all slapped fives at the finish and tried figuring out who would test the machine first.

Will asked, "How about we just go to the mall and ask people?"

"I'm telling you, we should try it on Mandy."

Neglected Nikki agreed, "She is the reason he came up with the idea."

"Call her."

"Wait," said Graves, "we should activate the machine first to make the slurpee to give to her, and then I'll call her over."

"Hold on, explain how this thing works again," said Neglected Nikki.

"Well, first we need some killer ice," and they poured some in before turning it on. "Then, you type in the name of your crush and their birthday, and then your name and your birthday."

As the machine began to mix, she asked, "What does it need your birth date for?"

"Numerology," said Will, "It sets him apart from every other Graves out there."

"So, then what?"

A nylon cup appeared below its dispenser before Graves explained, "Every ingredient mixed in the slurpee boosts oxytocin in the brain, releasing it into the bloodstream and increasing the hormone levels so high that doctors would need a million spinal tap methods to measure it."

"What happens if someone else drinks it?"

"They can't," he said, "because nylon produces static electricity causing killer shocks to anyone who touches it."

"Except the two people put into the *system*," said Will.

While on the phone, Mandy cursed Graves out for not returning her messages. After offering her a bonus if she agreed to babysit Davey, he was confidant she would come over.

"Gosh, I hope this works," said Will, before there was a knock at the door.

Mandy stormed in saying, "Where's my *fucking* money?"

"Relax, killer."

"Thirsty?" asked Neglected Nikki.

Graves handed her the slurpee and said, "it's tasty," and she drank it before her eyes widened.

"Well, hey there, Graves," she said. "You know, I always loved how smart you are."

Part 8: Love

Woman Supreme was jogging when she waved at The Mowing Man as he was cutting Gentleman Craig's grass.

The Mowing Man thought, "That's one fine Black woman."

Neglected Nikki and Will appeared pulling The Crazy Cupid Machine down the sidewalk in a wagon.

"We promised him," she told him.

"Well, I don't trust him."

She shouted to The Mowing Man, "Over here, sir!"

He stopped mowing and said, "Where's your other ol' friend?!"

"Busy?!" she said.

"Working?"

"Not quite," said Will.

He said, "Oh, they used to call it the ol' hanky panky or shaking the sheets if you know what I mean," and pushed his lawnmower onto the sidewalk.

"Wait, where are you going?"

"The cul-de-sac," and they followed him as he sang.

He placed another note in Woman Supreme's mailbox when Neglected Nikki reminded him about their time spent in the woods. The Mowing Man remembered their promise and followed their lead as Woman Supreme ran towards her home.

"How was your workout?" asked Will.

"Rejuvenating," she said, catching her breath.

"Thirsty?" asked Neglected Nikki.

"You can say that again."

"Well, we're selling slurpees," said Will. "Would you like to try a free sample?"

"Sure," she said, opening her garage.

He plugged it in and said, "We will just need your birthday to get started."

"It's a personal slurpee," Neglected Nikki told her, while Will entered it into the system.

With residue on her lips, Woman Supreme said, "Well, how's it hanging, mower amazing?"

"I imagine your love is more amazing," he said, "like the feel of wet grass beneath my bare feet."

Will unplugged the machine and said, "Well, looks like our work here is done."

Neglected Nikki kissed him.

Part 9: Machine

Graves walked in on his two friends undressing each other and kissing on Will's bed, which was covered in notes for the machine. They rushed to put their clothes back on, assuming he was Uncle Moe returning from another art auction downtown. When Graves flopped in the chair and removed his sunglasses, Will rushed to the kitchen for the first aid kit while Neglected Nikki blew on his scar.

"What happened?" she asked.

"It wore off, and she pounded me," he said.

Will returned also with a slab of meat and said, "Rub some of this ointment on it, and then slap this over your eye," and he did.

"It only lasts for a few weeks," said Graves.

"But it works," she said.

"Yea, it can still sell!" and there was a knock.

"Where's the machine?" asked Graves.

"It's in the garage." said Neglected Nikki.

Meanwhile, Will was standing with the front door open.

The Mowing Man smiled hiding his teeth and said, "I moved in."

"Uh, well, don't get too comfortable. You know how women are," he said.

"I just wanted to come by to say thank you."

"No problem," said Will. "Well, goodbye," and he closed the door.

The dropout wiped his brow and paced back and forth in his bedroom worried about whether Woman Supreme would reject The Mowing Man after the effect wore off. He suggested they offer Woman Supreme another slurpee to sustain her oxytocin levels and the others agreed. When they went to the garage with a warning label to put over the dispenser. the machine was missing.

"Nikki, you left the garage open?!" exclaimed Graves.

"Who could've taken it?" she asked.

They said, "The Mowing Man!"

Part 10: Where?

The Dropouts stood outside Woman Supreme's house after Will banged on the door begging for a brawl with The Mowing Man whose lawnmower was laying sideways on her lawn. Graves went over to it and began kicking the motor until oil leaked onto his shoe. Neglected Nikki tried calming them down before Woman Supreme opened the door tipsy off wine.

"May I help you?"

Will exclaimed, "Your boyfriend stole our machine!"

"This has to be a misunderstanding."

"Look, lady, just tell us where he is!" Graves exclaimed.

"Just who are you referring to?"

They said, "The Mowing Man!"

"Perhaps some wine can calm you three down while I tell you," said Woman Supreme, going into the kitchen for cups.

They followed her inside when Will said, "We don't want any wine, we want our machine back," and she poured some anyway.

"Well, he had me drop him off at the mall with it. Said he wanted to spread some love, which I think is quite admirable," she said, handing them their cups.

They thought, "Where?"

"Did he say where he was going to go after he left the mall?"

"Yes," she said, "to the rail."

Graves told his friends, "He's going to sell it to a company in Major City to get his life back!" and they rushed out the house.

The Dropouts hopped inside Graves' car with The Mowing Man's lawnmower and made a plan. Will and Neglected Nikki were going to search the mall while Graves parked at the rail, assuming The Mowing Man would appear on foot. When Graves drove up to the food court to let out his friends, they saw people kissing in the open and cuddled close together as they walked.

"Alright, let's split up."

"Let's just let it go! You guys can build something better!"

Will exclaimed, "No!" and got out.

Story 3
What Happens At
Venoa Beach Mall

Part 1: Vipers

With his feet up in Security, Officer Tod thought, "Where is everyone getting those slurpees from?" and rewound the footage.

The Mowing Man was spotted pulling The Crazy Cupid Machine around the mall in the wagon, stopping at nearby outlets to serve people in twos. Officer Tod saw him leave with others behind him begging for more before he noticed keys lying on a table. He rushed to The Food Court as The Scooter Crew rode past doing tricks for cheers, and pulled out his two-way radio to tell Supervisor Sam to unlock The Lost and Found.

"Do you have them in your hand?" asked his supervisor over the radio.

"Yea!"

"Does it have a car remote attached to it?"

"Yup," he said.

Supervisor Sam laughed and said, "Sound the alarm to see what car they're driving. We can get the license plate number and have Sheriff Shawn come look them up, roger that?"

"10-4," said Officer Tod, before running into Rosemary on skates.

She said, "Oh, I'm so sorry, officer! I have clients waiting and no time to order lunch," and fixed his collar.

He blushed, "No worries, you captivating cutie with piercings that scream 'make me hurt.'"

"Uh, thanks for the compliment?" and she skated in line at Fred's Chicken.

Officer Tod went outside where people sat listening to music on the mall's loudspeaker while trying on new clothes for the second time. After shopping until they could see the bottom of their wallets, they rested. The security guard walked past them and into the parking lot before sounding the alarm. When he found the car on the far end, he noticed stylish flip-flops, tiny bikinis, and inside out trunks with the drawstring missing in the backseat, as if the driver was back from Venoa Beach. After jotting down the license plate number, he looked on the bumper for stickers, assuming the car belonged to a teenager enjoying their break with their friends.

"Venoa Beach High Vipers," he read aloud, before going back inside where he sat at the bar for a beer.

"Hey, officer," said Cindy from Venoa Lakes, who appeared with the rest of The Makeup Misses and her boyfriend.

"What do you girls want?"

"My boyfriend wanted to know if you could buy him a drink, but don't worry because he literally drinks all the time, he's a bang buster."

Part 2: The Makeup Misses

Cindy's boyfriend stood in line at Chuck's Cheese Steaks while she was frolicking with her friends at the table as they ate Fred's Chicken. The boys in bunches blew kisses at the blondes, who ignored them, touching up their blush for the baddest guys in older gaggles. When one of the mature males made their mark on them with compliments and a casual invite to drink downtown, the three girls texted each other black hearts as if they were sitting apart.

"Don't tell Danny, but us three are literally going."

Erica said, "And we're going to get wasted with men."

"Literally," said Liz, while in the mirror of her makeup kit, "and maybe Cindy will find a real bad boy."

Erica laughed.

"Danny's parents may be religious, but there's a bad boy inside him that only a miss like me can fine tune to perfection," she said, picking at Erica's fries.

"Only time will tell."

Liz said, "Well, when that time comes, don't be shy to share him."

"I won't need to," Cindy replied, "when he'll literally be bad enough to use his boldness to blanket any babe he wants to at night because I am." She sipped Liz's soda and said, "He's gotta learn how to play the game."

"Maybe college will help him," said Erica.

"Who needs college when you've got The Makeup Misses?"

"We're literally a 101," said Liz.

"Let's practice."

They stuck their chests out and bit the bottom of their lips while batting their long eyelashes in the mirrors of their makeup kits. With their brushes in their hand, they waved at the boys before showing off their bare legs in open-toe heels that they only wore outside of school for the older guys who paid for them. Liz pulled out her lighter to burn the word "trust" Erica spelled out on a napkin. On another, Cindy wrote "us" and put a heart around it before they purred.

Danny came to the table with a loaded tray and said, "What did I miss?"

They laughed and said, "The Makeup Misses."

Cindy said, "Sneak into the bathroom with me, so I can show you what you missed," and he followed her with cheese hanging from his lip and a loose belt buckle howling.

Part 3: Bad

The Makeup Misses split up in Allison's Accessories, dropping items in their purses at the slightest sign that her employees were unaware. Danny followed behind Cindy, holding her purse open while Erica and Liz danced with themselves to appear like average teenage girls accustomed to accessorizing. As more came in, the more unsuspecting they were as Liz stopped to salute herself in the store mirror, holding up a pair of earrings to her ear that she tucked in her blouse. To further their illusion, Erica stood in line to pay for a lace glove that made older women wonder at its design.

"Where did you find that?" one asked.

"They're literally all out," she lied. "Besides, I don't want you wearing what we wear."

"Who's we?"

Cindy and Liz appeared before they all said, "The Makeup Misses."

"Well, who does your makeup? All women share beauty secrets," the woman said.

"The Makeup Misses," they said again.

"Do you ladies have a business card, or do you work in the mall?" she asked, assuming they were older.

"We literally work here," Liz lied.

"Yea, meet us at Vianny's in an hour for a touch up," said Erica.

"We'll make that man of yours at home beg you to the bedroom."

"Or bathroom," said Cindy, with Danny's arms around her waist.

Erica sat the lace glove on the counter and cracked a smile for Allison who greeted her with a gift card. After paying with cash from working on her father's yacht, Erica swiped a bracelet on display and said her goodbye. They walked with their heads high out of the store before stopping at a bench to laugh.

"So, where to next?" said Liz, and Cindy pointed to Lucy's Lingerie making Danny howl.

Lucy diverted products from a high-end beauty supply store in Major City to start a charity against abortion. Since then, she has raised a million dollars.

As Liz and Erica walked, flipping their hair as arrogant adolescence with above average looks, the couple followed behind them kissing like no one was watching. A boy from school noticed the two single girls and asked for one's phone number. They laughed in his face and then apologized with a double kiss on the cheek. When Danny picked Cindy up, holding her by her thighs to show off for the boy, Officer Tod appeared to impose his way of showing girls a good time.

"You hold her hand to make her feel wanted," he said, "like this," and demonstrated.

"Yea, well, she prefers kissing," said Danny, so the couple kissed again.

Part 4: Kissable

Before stepping foot inside Lucy's Lingerie, Cindy admired the three-piece set on the mannequin in the window, pulling her phone out to take a picture before recording herself praising it on camera. Liz saluted the set while Erica posed like the plastic person.

They were huddled up with their heels in hand when Liz said, "We might have to literally run out."

Erica opened her purse and said, "I literally need a bigger pocketbook."

"I'm literally not leaving the mall without that set," said Cindy, "because that mannequin literally looks kissable," and they stayed close together to shop.

They began with the table pieces, holding each one up in the light to see the design. There were sensors on all of them preventing the pricey girls from balling an item up and stuffing it in their purses. The Makeup Misses looked around to see if the racks and the wall pieces were also secure and they were. Cindy saw Danny roaming the store alone when she realized that he was the key to their scheme on clothes that made their teenage bodies kissable to older boys. She scurried over to him and asked for his pocketknife that he gave to her while giggling at the girl wearing lingerie in a picture. Cindy met with her friends at the racks where they began pulling items to try on, noticing the fitting rooms were unattended. They went back to the tables and tucked thongs in their skirts and bras before Lucy appeared as if she saw them.

"Finding everything okay, ladies?"

Cindy said, "Sure! But, uh, how much is that three-piece in the window?"

"That's part of our newest collection, so two hundred dollars before tax," she said and smiled.

"Why are you smiling? That price is literally ridiculous."

"Well, do you want your boyfriend to look at you and drool, or look at you like you're a fool?" Lucy asked, frowning.

"Was that supposed to be a sales pitch, you bitch?" as Erica and Liz eased their way to the fitting rooms.

"Now, that's no way to speak to a woman whose job is to make women like you feel sexy, now is it?"

Cindy flipped her hair and replied, "I literally always feel sexy," and stormed off.

Liz stood outside the fitting room whistling when Cindy slid the pocketknife underneath the door to Erica who pulled apart the sensor, holding onto the pieces to hide them in the store. The blonds took turns in the fitting room before Danny came over and began howling, drawing attention to the trio. Lucy made her way to where they stood with empty hangers and offered them a discount, suspecting they were trying to steal.

"Five percent?" asked Liz.

"That's literally nothing," said Erica.

"We'll take it," said Cindy. "Now, let me try on the one on display."

Lucy mocked them and said, "That's literally the last one, but I can order yours for an additional fee," and she smiled.

"*Why are you smiling*?" and the girls walked away.

After checking the size of the three-piece set on display, Cindy paced back and forth outside the store while Erica and Liz were finding spots to put the sensors inside.

Officer Tod appeared and said, "Now, how does a beautiful face like yours where a frown so cold?"

Cindy thought, "He's kissable. Maybe I can use him to get what I want," and she looked at his crotch and smiled at his eyes.

"You see, now, that's the kind of smile that turns a black heart bright red."

"Literally?" she said.

"Affirmative," he told her.

Cindy asked, "Well, what does my smile do to *your* heart?" and he squinted at her.

Part 5: Red

Officer Tod took Cindy on a tour of the mall, showing her the security camera's blind spots and recalling incidents that happened that made him a hero. Cindy batted her blue eyes at him and asked questions to seem interested. When he answered, she would bite her lip as if she was turned on by the details.

"Literally?" she kept saying.

Officer Tod pulled her close to avoid collision as The Scooter Crew rode by after slapping fives with Supervisor Sam, who appeared out of Vianny's.

She whispered, "Close, but not close enough," and Officer Tod looked into her eyes.

"Tod," said Supervisor Sam, "I need you to close all the exits in the corridors before lunch, it's supposed to rain, and we don't want any water leaking in, roger that?"

"10-4," he gulped, avoiding eye contact as Cindy held her tongue above her upper lip.

"Pretty woman," said Supervisor Sam and walked away.

"People don't shop in the corridor," said Cindy, and they walked towards the first one making eye contact at every turn.

Meanwhile, Erica and Liz were inside Kim's Nail Salon picking out colors for their hands and feet while laughing at the girls in school who they saw roaming the mall. They stole a few small bottles of polish before choosing the purple one.

"No, no, no," said Kim, who committed bankruptcy fraud by withholding assets to giveaway to the less fortunate, "go extreme."

"Purple is literally the color of royalty," said Liz.

"My dear, you're not a queen yet."

"Literally, make your suggestion, lady," said Erica.

Kim got some polish and said, "Here, go with red, a symbol of confidence."

"Look at us," said Liz, "does it look like we need a confidence boost?"

"I can't see you with all that makeup on," she said, leaving the red polish in front of them.

As the technician filed their nails, she said, "Red is also associated with love. Seductive love. Doesn't every woman want a man to want them for who they are, not just what they look like?"

Danny peeked in and asked, "Have you two seen Cindy?"

Part 6: Seduction

"This is the last corridor," said Officer Tod.

"I never knew there were literally so many doors at the mall."

With his hands in his pockets, he said, "Well, what's something that I never knew about you, since I see you here all the time."

"Well, you never knew I wore these," and she lifted the back of her skirt to show her thong.

He gulped and told her, "No, no, I didn't."

"Touch it," and he squinted at her as Supervisor Sam appeared at the other end.

"All secure?!"

"Yes, sir," said Officer Tod, walking towards him with Cindy behind him rolling her eyes.

Meanwhile, Danny walked into Bryan's Barbershop that was ran by Latino owner Bryan, who uses money from cryptojacking to pay for school supplies for the entire freshman class each year and was finishing Haywood's hair. Danny recognized The Bass Boys as the rest of them played pool and turned around to leave, tripping over his feet. Blake called him out before he could stand up straight.

"I always thought The Bang Busters was a cool name," he said.

"Yea, man, how you been?"

Danny looked confused.

"Don't leave," said Fish, "when you haven't gotten a haircut. I'll help you pick a style that's guaranteed to seduce the girls. Check these out," and he showed him the chart on the wall.

"I have a girlfriend," he said.

"I had muchas chicas in high school," said Bryan, "and the first one I fell in love with ended up cheating on me."

Blake blurted, "Hey, Haywood, look who showed up?"

"It's The Bang Busters," he said. "Hey, tell Bobby I said what's up."

Danny left.

Part 7: Show

Rosemary sat at her computer conspiring with hackers to steal corporate data from companies in Major City to sell and pay for a car for Homeless Man Twenty who lived on the paved trail. When Liz and Erica walked in to watch the television she left on to lure new clientele, she minimized the screen and spun around on her skates to impress them into buying. The two makeup misses clapped for her before suggesting she discount her services for them for the sake of womanhood.

"Sorry, I need the money," said Rosemary.

"We can literally bring you customers," said Liz.

"Let's make a business arrangement," said Erica. "A free tattoo today, a slew of new clients tomorrow?"

"Sorry, but if we're going to do that, it would have to be the other way around. New clients tomorrow, a free tattoo the next day?"

"That works," they said.

Erica suggested, "How about you pierce my belly button now for Liz here to touch up your makeup to seal the deal?"

"That works," said Rosemary.

Meanwhile, Officer Tod walked Cindy back to Lucy's Lingerie assuming her friends would find her there. She rolled her eyes at the sight of Lucy still inside standing behind the register before coming up with a plan to continue seducing Officer Tod until he gave in. She turned off her phone in her purse without pulling it out as Danny called for the sixth time.

"I can't find my phone," she said, searching her purse.

"Maybe someone found it and turned it in."

Supervisor Sam appeared and said, "Making her feel safe?"

"She lost her phone, sir."

He laughed and said, "I hate when that happens. Here are the keys to The Lost and Found. I'm taking a lunch downtown, and you're in charge," walking away.

They went to the closed door of Security, passing The Scooter Crew who parked their scooters in The Food Court while eating gyros from Kristen's Gourmet. He opened the door before asking her to wait outside. Officer Tod was wiping his brow, struggling to open the chest when Cindy came in closing the door behind her.

She locked it and said, "Are you a real Venoan man?" and she took off her blouse before saying, "I don't want you to say anything, I want you to watch me until you're ready to show me."

Cindy sat in a chair and stretched her long leg out pointing her toes before untying her heels with her tongue on her upper lip. She told him to take them off before standing tall to bend over. After lifting her skirt all the way up and twirling her bra on her finger, she sat again flipping her hair as she was spreading her legs. Cindy closed them after purring and stood to remove her thong.

With her head high and hands on her hips, she looked into his eyes and said, "Take me," and he did.

Part 8: Took

Officer Tod stood with Cindy outside of Lucy's Lingerie after they walked there without mentioning the mess they made in Security. He asked her about returning to school to reign as a senior among the boldest students who saw her as prime. She told him she was running for senior class president before Lucy walked out the store and came back.

"So, how was it?" Cindy asked him.

"Call me," he said, pulling out his business card.

She snatched it and said, "Wouldn't you like to see me in this?" and stood by the display.

"Who wouldn't?" said Officer Tod.

"Then, buy it for me for a *night* with me," and he pulled out his wallet before she took it and stormed inside.

Meanwhile, Erica and Liz took pictures with Rosemary, each posing in their own way as The Scooter Crew rode inside with their helmets hanging from their necks. Rosemary warned Scott that her brother Mike, who was leader of The Skate Lords, would do anything for his title as Venoa Extreme Champion. The boys laughed as they stocked up on candy from her dish and lounged around. Erica took more pictures with

Rosemary before Danny appeared out of Roger's Electronics across from them bragging about stealing batteries.

"One pack of batteries?" said Erica.

"You're literally pathetic."

Part 9: Roger That

Lucy prepared to leave the store to her proud employees who were all females, except one named Roy, who wore a tie as the others worked in skirt suits. The owner counted the drawers and refolded items on the tables while Roy rehung tops loose in the fitting rooms. As Lucy was vacuuming the shelves, Roy found a piece of a sensor in the pocket of a top. He rushed over to tell Lucy whose vacuum was clogged from sucking up loose screws. After she detached the vacuum to count them, she stormed over to the counter to call Supervisor Sam who laughed on his way to see.

Over the radio, Supervisor Sam said, "Tod, I need you to check cameras on level two, rewinding back about two hours when some young women reportedly stole clothing from Lucy's Lingerie, roger that?" as he walked in.

Meanwhile, Cindy appeared at Rosemary's Tattoo Parlor.

"You literally won't believe what I got," and she showed her friends the three-piece set.

Erica asked, "How?"

"Yea, you gotta' tell us the story," said Liz.

"Later," she said.

They took pictures of Cindy holding up her new lingerie and posing like the girls in the pictures hanging in Lucy's store. Danny sat squinting at his girlfriend, who was so excited she ignored him as he opened the batteries, tossing each one in the air and catching it. As the girls were talking, Officer Tod appeared.

"Roger, that," he said over the radio and waited.

Cindy said, "Tod, come take a picture with us."

"Step out here, it's better lighting," and they did.

As Sheriff Shawn walked towards them with Supervisor Sam and Lucy close behind, Cindy squinted at Officer Tod while she and her two friends took off their heels and ran.

Part 10: Chase

The Makeup Misses started towards Vianny's pushing people out their way and snatching makeup and perfume on display. As Sheriff Shawn chased them, Supervisor Sam hoped to cut them off by running the other way. The girls swung open the doors to the parking lot on the opposite side to where Liz was parked. They were hiding inside a cargo bed when Sheriff Shawn appeared in the parking lot out of breath. As he stood with his back turned still on the radio, the girls got out and ran up the steep hill into a larger parking lot.

"You parked upstairs!" Erica exclaimed, and they ran back into the mall where they hid in a fitting room on the top floor of Vianny's. After catching their breath, they walked out and swiped dresses to change into before walking into Dee Dee's Shoes and picking out sneakers.

"Oh, these are cute," said Cindy.

"Literally," said Liz, and they walked out before scurrying to The Food Court.

Officer Tod stood at the exit as the girls were running towards it. When Cindy blew him a kiss, he stepped out of their way. They sprinted to the car before driving off with Cindy waving out the window.

Meanwhile, Sheriff Shawn escorted Danny, who was in handcuffs, to Security where Supervisor Sam stood with Becca.

"Tod," he said over the radio, "where did you put those set of keys you found earlier today? She went all the way home to...," and he asked Becca, "Where did you say you live again?"

"Venoa Crossing."

Story 4
Neighbors Of
Venoa Crossing

Part 1: Lost

Butch was barking as Becca walked in the house.

"Mom, I'm back from the mall!" she shouted and ran upstairs to her room.

Her mother was motionless on the bed when Becca nudged her. Assuming she was asleep, Becca took the open book on her mother's chest and began to read to her while sitting at the foot of the bed. When she heard Dr. Brent come in with strangers echoing throughout the house, she looked down from the loft. Medics were coming up the stairs with a stretcher causing her to stir.

"What are you doing to my mom!"

Dr Brent said, "She's gone, Becca."

"No, she's not! She's sleeping!" and she cried.

He embraced her and said, "Everything's going to be fine."

She pushed him away and yelled, "Seriously? Dad, you don't know what it's like to be a teenage girl!"

"You've learned as much as you were supposed to from her," as the medics were coming down the stairs.

"Where are you guys taking her?!" pulling one by their shirt with her father holding her waist. "Mom, can you hear me?! I'm lost without you!" and they lowered the wheels, rolling her out the front door and into the ambulance.

As they drove away, Becca rushed to her car, pulled out the driveway, and parked at Preacher Paul's house where First Lady sat in the window reading scripture.

Part 2: Scripture

First Lady opened the door wearing a veil with band aids on her toes from praising in her heels. She was as proud to show off her worn out pages of scripture as she was to be a woman. With tears flowing, Becca put her head on her shoulder and recited The Lord's Prayer.

"And the women said 'Amen,'" said the old soul, running her fingers through Becca's hair.

As she walked her to the sofa, the teenager said, "I can't believe she's gone."

"Disease is nothing but the devil, but you cry, cry like Hannah, who did so profusely, that she made a promise to the Lord that changed her life."

"Seriously? she said, wiping her tears. "Can you tell me more about her?"

"She was faithful, devoted her son to the Lord, but when she cried, a *man* told her she was drunk, but she kept praying," said First Lady with her hand on Becca's thigh. "I'm going to get you some water."

"With ice, please."

"Oh no," said First Lady, "living water, the words of the Lord in scripture," and she went into Preacher Paul's study for a Bible. "Remember, the fear of the Lord is the beginning of knowledge."

"But Venoans don't fear consequences."

"Sure, we don't," she said and smiled, moving the hair from Becca's face and tucking it behind her ear. She licked her lips from behind the veil and blushed as the button on her blouse became undone. First Lady closed it and said, "To fear the Lord is to reverence Him. That means to respect Him and admire Him."

Becca looked at her and said, "Why doesn't scripture just say that?"

"His ways are not like our ways, just read," said First Lady, as Preacher Paul drove up in an SUV with the windows down. He backed in the driveway and stepped out with sunblock on his nose, wearing basketball shorts and shades with a cross hanging from his gold chain. He dribbled two basketballs to the front door before going inside where the two females sat with their thighs touching reading scripture aloud.

He interrupted saying, "What's up, y'all?" and Becca greeted him with a hug.

"She's mourning," said First Lady, "so she needs the hug, not you."

"When, today?" he asked Becca.

"She doesn't need your sympathy. Her mother was God's child, and to be absent from the body is to be present with the Lord."

Becca said, "Seriously?"

Part 3: Children

By the pond in the neighborhood was where people gathered to remember Becca's mother. Most were neighbors of Venoa Crossing who rolled out of bed. Others were hospital staff or one of Becca's friends like Jessica, who sat on the Bible after many were passed around. Two children chased each other in circles around a tattooed Latino named Angel as The Godfather mingled.

"I don't think funerals are that bad, do you?" asked a smart child.

The Godfather said, "You know, for a Venoan, a funeral is not a waste."

"Why do you think it isn't, sir?"

"Venoans live their lives fully as God allows," he said, "because to fear consequences for your actions is to fear living itself."

Everyone sat while Dr. Brent stood behind the podium. He welcomed them before Preacher Paul presided.

"Uh, we're all God's children," he said, "and He has seen this woman's work, and so she is in Heaven, in a mansion."

Meanwhile, Haywood was skimming through scripture.

"A mansion in the sky? Where's that at?"

"Man, put that book down."

"God's children?" asked Fish. "So, that means I'm a god, if He's the Father, right? Like Father like son?"

Blake said, "Right. *You're* in control of your life."

First Lady yelled, "Hallelujah!"

"Now, there's an outburst," said Fish.

"Man, I bet she can't spell it."

Haywood was reading when he said, "It says here, that God's children are peculiar. She's just being herself."

"Man, give me that," closing the book.

"Peculiar? Do you know how many girls we would get if we were strange? Zero."

After Preacher Paul's eulogy, Dr. Brent kissed his wife and closed the casket.

Becca thought, "I will always be her baby girl."

Part 4: Baby

Before Blake could open the car door for her, Becca hopped out and ran into his arms. She whispered something in his ear when Blake told her to jump, catching her by her thighs and carrying her through the garage.

He kicked open the door and asked, "Where's your, Dad?"

"Saving lives," she said, kissing him.

Blake said, "Slow down," going upstairs.

"Seriously? I yearn for you."

"You're vulnerable right now. I don't want to feel like I'm taking advantage of you."

She pushed him on her bed and shouted, "Take advantage of me!" and he grabbed a condom off the nightstand.

"We won't be needing that anymore," she said, throwing it across the room.

Blake said, "Time out," and stood up.

"Seriously?"

"Well, no, but *yes*! What if you get pregnant?"

"Having a baby is the whole point of having sex!"

"No, it isn't!"

"Then, what else is it for?"

"Sex is self-expression! It brings out our personalities!"

"I just wanna feel the way my mom felt," she said, "and scripture says to be fruitful and multiply."

"I don't think that just means make babies," sitting beside her. "In the story, the first thing God did for Adam after creating him was he gave him a job. That was to be creative and use his imagination to name the animals. Being fruitful could also be about working hard to see the fruits of your labor."

"You have a job."

"Yea, but your world became dark after your mom passed. The only way to the light is to do what Adam did when *he* was lost, so get creative to cope, not crazy."

Meanwhile, Dr. Brent came in through the front door bearing gifts for Becca he bought from over-billing.

He shouted, "Rebecca!" before they came downstairs.

Becca reached for the shopping bags. Her father guarded them, laughing at her missing bra straps beneath her blouse. He handed her a laptop with music software to assist her recording, a microphone, and an SAT study guide. Blake sighed with relief after seeing several boxes of condoms through the plastic. When Dr. Brent gave Becca a five-hundred-dollar gift card, the two teenagers raced out the front door and into her car.

Part 5: Gift

The Godfather was holding Bible study a few houses down from Preacher Paul. Principal Jon was there, Woman Supreme showed up with a new man, and even Officer Tod came with plans to meet Cindy on the paved trail. When it was over, The Godfather and Mary took a walk around the neighborhood with their dog, who they took home from the pound. They helped construct the building with cash from selling counterfeit money. After running a remedial reading program for former gang members at the recreational center in Major City, The Godfather was given cases of it as a thank you from those troubled youth.

"God made those trees," he said to his wife.

"Pretty."

"Look up at the clouds," and she did.

"Glorious they are," said Mary.

"Only God could've made those."

"The sky is one lovely blue."

He laughed and said, "God chose that color."

They walked toward Dr. Brent's house where Becca sat inside her car singing with the windows down.

"Do you hear that, Daddy?" asked Mary.

"Sounds like a bird," said The Godfather. "You know, God made animals," as they approached the car.

"Oh, bless your heart, baby," said Mary to Becca, "but you have a lovely voice."

"Thank you."

"You know, God gave you that gift."

Becca smiled with tears flowing.

"Oh, there's no need for tears when you got a voice like yours that can evoke emotion from people, now is there, dear heart?"

Becca said, "Mom died."

"And she was a wonderful woman to have nurtured a daughter with such a gift."

"You know, people in scripture sang to God. He loves singing," said The Godfather, "and I would ask you to come by for worship, but you would have to know Him," and the couple walked away.

Angel appeared after Preacher Paul drove past, honking his horn at Becca, who was singing, waving a pen to the rhythm. She looked out the window at Angel, who was a reformed and refined gang member, joining as a youth after losing someone close. He walked over to her and smiled.

She asked, "Why are you so happy?"

Angel said, "Because life never stops?"

"We stop living when we're dead."

"What is death to you when you can record yourself singing, eliminating the chance of ever being forgotten?"

Becca said, "I sing at Gifts Church with First Lady."

Angel became more serious to say, "Music is emotional, so don't get confused should you continue to sing at places like that. For a church is just one building in a world that *es grande* like your gift is, *sí*?"

Part 6: Big

After having sex, Blake and Becca fell off her bed.

"Are you alright?" they asked each other, reaching for their clothes.

Becca started to sing as she scurried over to her desk where her notebook was left open on the surface.

"What are you working on?"

"A song about you," said Becca. "Do you wanna hear what I have so far?" She sang, "*Look into my eyes, with no fiery lies, and we'll die as dragonflies.*"

"What's it called?"

She said, "Dragonflies," and he tried singing it as well as she did, and she laughed.

"Don't forget about me when you make it big."

She sat on top of him and asked, "As big as your heart?"

"All my boys have big hearts."

"You mean The Bass Boys."

Jessica barged in saying, "You're not going to believe what's happening downtown!"

"Seriously? How did you get in?"

"Really? You told me your garage code, remember?" she said, before telling her The Riot, an alternative rock band from Venoa Cove was performing at Nakeela's Bar.

"Didn't they dropout of Venoa Beach High?" she asked.

"Yea, they're home schooled! But that's not the good news," she flipped her braids. "They're looking for a new lead singer!"

"Seriously?" said Becca.

"Isn't this big for you?" and she hugged her friend before winking at Blake who licked his lips.

Part 7: Seriously

After praise rehearsal, First Lady invited Becca over for dinner. The old soul lifted her veil to feed herself while watching Becca twirl her hair with her free hand. Preacher Paul's preteen daughter Reese listened to music on a pair of headphones, dancing in her chair and tapping her plate with her fork to keep the tempo.

First Lady said, "You led praise like prophetess Miriam herself."

"Thank you," said Becca, "but I'm thinking about quitting."

She dropped her fork and assumed, "God is displeased."

"Seriously?"

"Heaven is a place of worship. You should practice as much as you can. You don't wanna be the only one walking the streets of gold without a song to sing, now do you?"

Becca shook her head before explaining, "But there's a band that's looking for a lead singer, and I want to be it."

First Lady banged the table and exclaimed, "The devil's music! Be not conformed to this world, but be transformed by the renewing of your mind, Becca!"

"But the world is a wonderful place."

"No, it isn't!" and her veil fell off. "It's cold, *damn* cold I tell you!"

"Well, there has to be balance."

First Lady rushed to the bathroom as Preacher Paul walked in after overhearing their argument.

"Is everything cool?"

"I told her I was quitting the praise team to join a rock band."

"That's great," said Preacher Paul, hugging her.

First Lady returned hidden behind the veil.

Part 8: Hiding

Blake was fishing in the pond when Becca asked, "Have you ever met First Lady?" as she brushed Butch's fur.

"I caught something!" and he reeled it in.

Becca stared at the flapping fish saying, "It has whiskers."

"It's a channel catfish," said Blake, unhooking it. "Take a picture," and she did.

"Put it back in."

Holding the fish to his face, he looked it in its eyes and asked Becca, "Does your pastor eat fish?"

She shrugged and said, "I bet his wife does because the Lord fed thousands with two fish."

"How many times do I have to tell you that those stories in the Bible never happened? They're lessons."

Neighbors of Venoa Crossing rested near them, reaching for cold beer from a cooler with their eyes covered with shades and music playing through speakers. Among them was Angel, who jumped in the water and swam across, losing a boot that he floated to find before backstroking to shore. Becca waved to him.

"You may only live once!" he shouted.

As neighbors left the pond, leaving them alone with Angel who was making snow angels in the green grass, Blake put his arm around Becca and told her to sing to him and she did.

He gave her a locket saying, "This is your blessing for praising me."

"A locket?"

"When praises go up, blessings come down."

"Am I dating God Himself?"

"We're all like Him."

Becca scratched her head saying, "Tell that to First Lady."

"That woman at your church who wears a veil? She's hiding."

"She doesn't think I should join The Riot."

He exclaimed, "Church is holding you back!" and grabbed her by the hand with Butch's leech in the other.

While being pulled onto the sidewalk, Becca asked, "Where are we going?"

"Show me where she lives!"

Part 9: Live

Angel followed them beating on his chest and spitting, wiping his mouth with his wrist and curling his upper lip. The tattooed Latino started jumping on his toes, loosening his neck behind Becca as they waited outside Preacher Paul's house. First Lady opened the door with one Bible under her arm and another in her free hand.

Blake asserted himself saying, "Tell my girlfriend who you really are!"

"I've read scripture to Becca as my dear friend and encouraged her to go the Lord's way."

Angel shouted, "Tell her to live!"

"I said tell her what you are, not who you want to be!"

She laughed and said, "The Word says, as a woman thinketh in her heart, so is she."

Blake looked into her eyes asking, "Do you think in your heart, or do you *know* in your heart?"

She lifted her veil.

"Tell her to live!"

"Are you trying to confuse me like the damn devil himself? God is not the author of confusion."

Angel shouted, "Tell her to live!"

"You're the one confused. I see it in your eyes," he said. "Now, tell us what you really are."

"*Lesbian!*" exclaimed First Lady and slammed the door shut.

Part 10: Closer

Dr. Brent plugged his camera into his television and turned on old recordings of Becca singing. Before making a path to the living room from the front door with red towels, he put pictures of her and her mother on the kitchen table around a cake.

Blake walked in with Becca who asked, "Dad, why are there towels on the floor?"

"It's the red carpet," he said.

"Seriously?"

"Yea, you're nominated."

She said, "Dad, stop," and blushed, following the path to the living room.

When the recording showed Becca receiving the reward for first place, Blake clapped and carried her into the kitchen for cake.

"Dad, what did you do this for?"

Dr. Brent said, "Nothing," and smiled.

"So, are you ready?" Blake asked Becca.

She laughed and said, "First Lady says I should find a boyfriend that's going to bring me closer to the Lord."

"Who you need is somebody that's going to bring you closer to yourself, who you really are!"

"Who am I?"

"The next lead singer for The Riot!"

"We should invite Homeless Man Twenty to come with us."

Blake agreed.

Story 5
What Happens On
The Paved Trail

Part 1: Twenty

People parked their bikes to sit among others who trampled the trail on trikes as Homeless Man Twenty stood on a crate retelling The Rain. When he finished the story, they dropped dollars and coins in the hood of his coat and carried on. He stepped off the crate and combed his gray beard with his hands before counting the cash, licking his fingers. After separating all the coins, he washed his hands in a cup of water, removing the dirt under his fingernails.

As a man was walking past, he smiled for sympathy saying, "A dollar will do," and then frowned after being ignored.

Meanwhile, Blake and Becca spotted him.

"Alright, take your time," said Blake, and Becca walked over to him with her boyfriend close behind.

"Hey, Twenty!"

"I don't have any candy," he said.

"That doesn't mean you're not sweet. We've heard your stories." Blake stood on the crate mimicking him.

"So, you teenagers came to play, ay?" asked Homeless Man Twenty. "It's too bad the crate is not a toy."

Blake jumped off.

"No, sir," said Becca. "We seriously came to invite you downtown to see The Riot perform."

"With a name like The Riot, residents should be running from them, not racing to them."

Blake said, "So, is that a yes?"

He looked into her eyes and looked away saying, "*I don't dance,*" and covered his face with his coat.

Homeless Man Twenty peeked out as Becca walked away with Blake's arm around her shoulder. He reached for his notebook and began writing a story he titled "Teenagers." He spoke the words as he wrote them underneath his coat, waiting to be interrupted by a generous jogger with something to spare. When he finished writing, he laid on his back rehearsing.

Part 2: Laid

Rosemary said, "It's easy, like this," and spun around on her skates, laughing as The Makeup Misses were struggling on their own pair.

"I'm literally going to fall," said Liz, before she fell.

"Sorry!" exclaimed Rosemary, helping her stand.

Cindy said, "I bet if you taught that homeless man how to skate, it'll get him laid."

"There's something about a man on wheels that turns us girls on, right?" asked Erica.

"Twenty, on skates?" said Rosemary, as they skated to the crowd.

Homeless Man Twenty told his new story, making some laugh while lazing on the pavement with their shoes off. While The Makeup Misses were changing into their sneakers, Homeless Man Twenty cleared his throat distracted by the beautiful blonds as they bent over.

Everyone was scattered on the trail when Rosemary said, "Guess what, Twenty? I almost have enough for that car I promised you!"

"My license is expired."

"Sorry, we can get you a new one!"

"I like my picture on the one I have."

"Your next picture will be better because everyone literally looks better after they get laid," said Liz.

Homeless Man Twenty said, "I haven't gotten laid since..."

"Today," said Erica.

"Because we're literally going to help you."

Part 3: Help

Homeless Man Twenty returned to the paved trail showered and dressed in designer denim. The Makeup Misses turned his hat backwards and unbuttoned his shirt. They gave him gum and showed him how to walk like a young man, cool after his first cold beer.

As an older woman walked past, Erica said, "There's a good one."

"Remember what we taught you," said Liz.

He said, "Head straight, eyes straight, and be straight forward."

"You got it," they said.

"Now, go get her, tiger," said Cindy.

Homeless Man Twenty offered the older woman a stick of gum before complimenting her clothes.

"Ouch!" he exclaimed, after she tugged on his beard.

"It's not fake? But you're dressed so young,"

"Blame those teenage girls over there."

"Are those your granddaughters?"

"If I say yes, will that get you to sleep with me?" he asked.

She exclaimed, "You need help!" and slapped him.

As she walked away, he looked back at the girls as they scurried over to him in shock.

"Literally, what did you say?" Liz asked.

"I gave her a compliment," he said.

"On what?"

"Her capris," he said.

"Wrong!" said Erica.

Cindy said, "Next time, just tell her how attracted you are to her, and then just go for the kill!"

"There won't be a next time because my feelings are hurt. Would you girls mind taking me to Larry's Liquor Store on the state road, so I can wash down my pills?"

Part 4: Hurt

The Skate Lords tossed their helmets in the air, catching them on their heads at a moderate speed. They hopped over Homeless Man Twenty, who was lying in middle of the pavement, breathing into a brown paper bag. With tears flowing, Neglected Nikki scurried over to his side, pulling him by his pits back to his crate.

"You could've gotten hurt," she said, wiping her tears.

He sipped some liquor and said, "Another teenager, ay? Shouldn't you be getting ready for school?"

"I dropped out sophomore year."

"Well, that's too bad," said Homeless Man Twenty. "Do you mind telling me why?"

She said, "I'm a creative."

"Well, you made the right decision then. No one wants to learn what they don't want to learn." He sipped some more and asked, "Why are you crying?"

"Will broke up with me," crying on his shoulder.

"You're hurt. That's good. You're learning," he said, offering her some liquor. Neglected Nikki drank some and spit it out. "You should sip if you're not used to it," Twenty said.

After trying to keep up with him, she said, "I have to pee."

"There's a spot between the trees. C'mon, I'll take you there."

As they walked towards the woods, Homeless Man Twenty poured more liquor down her throat.

While urinating, she asked, "Is anybody watching?"

"Just me," he said, taking off his pants.

"What are you doing?!"

"Getting laid," he said, grabbing her by the waist.

Neglected Nikki scratched him and ran.

Part 5: Over

Cindy was checking the time on her phone and thought, "Where is he?"

Still with no word from Officer Tod, she searched for Homeless Man Twenty using the flashlight on her phone.

"Maybe he's seen him," she thought.

When she found the old man asleep, she took his coat and covered him.

He gripped her leg and said, "Back to see me, ay? I knew you liked older men with all that makeup on," putting his hand up her skirt.

"Stop it!" she screamed, before punching him in his face.

She ran down the paved trail in heels calling for Officer Tod. After catching up to her, Homeless

Man Twenty covered her mouth before taking her into the woods.

He pulled out a knife saying, "How about we see what you really look like without makeup on, ay?" as he began removing it with the edge.

She cried, "You're cutting my face!"

"It's almost over," he said. "Did you get lip injections? Because I can cut those off if you don't like them."

"I don't have lip injections!" she screamed.

"Good," he said and slit her throat.

Part 6: Cindy

The Bass Boys were walking around.

Blake said, "Were you guys watching her perform?"

"She did her thing, man."

Fish said, "She should change her name."

"How about Dragonfly like the song she wrote?" asked Haywood.

Blake was sniffing when he asked, "Do you guys smell that?" and they held their stomachs.

Fish said, "It's coming from the woods," following the odor with the others behind him. "Look, it's Cindy!"

The blond who basked in attention from boys brainwashed by her beauty was covered in dry blood from her neck to her chin. The Bass Boys were reminded of the number of boys who walked out Venoa Beach High sulking after being rejected by her. She would give them air kisses to appear approachable and applaud them, thanking each one for the ego boost.

Blake said, "Maybe Homeless Man Twenty knows something?"

"It's Cindy, man. Just leave her."

Part 7: Dead

After passing by The Bass Boys, Will said, "He's dead when I see him."

"It's my fault," said Neglected Nikki, coughing behind a mask.

"You should still be in quarantine like he should've been!"

Neglected Nikki said, "He was drunk!"

"That's no excuse!" he shouted, looking around.

Homeless Man Twenty was nowhere in sight.

"Where is he?"

"Will, I could die. Aren't I more important than your revenge?"

Staring cold into her eyes, he assured her that the homeless man would be remembered as a myth without a memorial to show otherwise.

Part 8: Memorial

Officer Tod was consoling The Makeup Misses as many gathered to honor Cindy. As Preacher Paul spoke, The Bass Boys stood away from the crowd with Pickney, who was without Tucker for appearances.

"Uh, and let this be a reminder," he said, "that life as a Venoan is always at risk."

Jessica tapped Blake on the shoulder.

"Hey, where's Becca?" he asked.

"Harry's house in Venoa Cove."

"She's in?"

"You're now dating the lead singer for The Riot! But who knows for how much longer."

Story 6
Neighbors Of
Venoa Cove

Part 1: Heart Race

As sweat dripped onto their instruments, The Riot breathed heavy in the open garage.

Harry shouted, "Dragonflies, on three!" and counted.

While singing, Becca ran her fingers through her hair with her eyes closed. With an extra pick in his mouth, Mitch played the melody on his lead guitar. Bran pointed his bass in the air from the floor, as he improvised on his knees. Harry tossed his drumsticks and caught them in time to keep the tempo. When the song ended, the boys slapped fives and poured water on their heads.

"That's how you practice, dude!" exclaimed Mitch.

"Perfection, dude," said Bran.

"Seriously."

"Now, for Heart Race," said Harry. "Becca, you do the ad-libs on this one."

When he started to sing, Becca blushed, looking back at him for her cues. She danced out of her shoes. The boys wore their wet shirts half on. Becca tied her hair in a ponytail in between singing as Harry swung his, getting sweat on his symbols. When the song ended, Mitch put Becca on his shoulders.

"Who's that song about?" she asked.

"It's about this girl I met at Nakeela's Bar."

"Me?" she asked, blushing again.

"Smile, and I'll prove it," and she did. "Now, feel my chest."

With her hand over his heart, Becca said, "You're serious."

Part 2: The Real

Beyond the woods was a small, sheltered inlet where The Real hung out, having sessions of smoking hashish. As a conscious rap group who took the rail to Major City for school, they thrived in harsh settings, honing their social skills to inspire their songs. They planned to earn the stage at The Festival after Becca outshined them at Nakeela's Bar.

120

Jazzy passed the blunt and said, "That white girl can sing, honey," blowing smoke.

"Look," said Mirror, exhaling, "even with my best beats, they're a tough act to follow."

Curiosity commented, "We're not an act. This is real to us."

"Do you think they'll really put their performance on the line to prove what they've already proven to us?" asked Jazzy.

"We're not asking them to. We're demanding they do."

Big Ant appeared at the cove, yo-yoing with his book of rhymes. He flashed some cash from cashiering to encourage Mirror to discount his beats for him. When he did, the six-foot-six Bass Boy rushed back to his grandmother's house in the neighborhood to tell her.

Part 3: Recording

Big Ant was recording in the walk-in closet rapping about girls when she shouted from downstairs, "Grandbaby!"

"Yes, grandma!"

"Your food is getting cold!"

"Coming, grandma!"

"I want you take Winner out for a walk after you're done!

He came downstairs asking, "Man, why do *I* have to?"

"You will do what your grandmamma tells you."

With a pair of wireless headphones over his ears, he ate some and gave the rest to Winner. Big Ant took him outside as some neighbors were parking and a few were walking for exercise. When Winner stopped near Harry's house to pee, Big Ant saw the drummer lying on the grass with Becca on top of him. He was recording them when Latina Selena walked past jump roping.

He shouted, "Wait!" removing his headphones.

"Que? Soy buena. Mirror is my boyfriend."

"But are you worth fighting for?"

"Si."

"Then, walk with me," and she did.

Part 4: Fight

The Real drove past.

"Look, that's my girl," with his head out window.

"With the big homie?" asked Curiosity, turning the car around.

Mirror hopped out and said, "She's mine."

Big Ant ignored him saying, "I have your number, so call you later?"

"Yo no se," she said.

"Her number?!" exclaimed Mirror, grabbing Big Ant by the arm.

Big Ant swung his fist before landing the next punch. Mirror shook off the blow and body punched him to his knees.

He walked over to his girlfriend and said, "Your time's up," and left her standing.

Part 5: Time

After recording in his basement, Curiosity was confident they could get a record deal following a performance at The Festival.

"It's time," he told Mirror.

"Look, are you sure?"

He said, "Listen," and opened his bedroom window for them to hear The Riot rehearsing.

Mirror said, "Go get the car!" tossing Jazzy his keys.

Meanwhile, The Riot sang their last song.

"You know what we need?" asked Harry.

"Joy ride!" they all said, before getting in Becca's car.

As they drove away, The Real parked across from Harry's house.

"We missed them," said Jazzy.

Curiosity said, "I have a better idea," and crept into the open garage with Mirror behind him. "Let's get the speakers."

"What about the microphones?"

"Those, too," he whispered, before leaving a note on the snare.

Part 7: Cove

The Real waited for The Riot to appear at the cove.

"There they go," said Curiosity.

They made their way through the woods when Harry asked, "What do you guys want from us?"

"Your spot in The Festival."

"Seriously? How is that possible?"

"We'll have a concert on the cul-de-sac. The whole neighborhood will vote."

"Dude, what if there's a tie?" asked Bran.

Mirror said, "Then, we'll post it online."

"Whoever gets the most likes performs at The Festival," said Jazzy.

Harry said, "You're on," and they all shook hands.

After sharing a blunt with them, The Riot boys walked away with their equipment.

Part 8: Free

As Becca and Jazzy went door to door passing out fliers, The Yearning Man parked at his new home in a moving truck. With the radio blasting, he sang. He was a white man with a goatee he maintained with a toothbrush. As a painter, The Yearning Man painted over every trespassing sign in Major City to allow homeless men places to post.

Becca rushed over to him exclaiming, "Free concert, sir!"

He read the flier and said, "Well, I yearn for music. Do you know why?"

"Why, sir?" they asked.

"Music sets you free."

"So, then you'll come," asked Jazzy.

"If you ladies yearn to perform, then I yearn to be there."

Part 9: Yearning

"She sings amazingly!" dancing with Fish in the crowd. While recording video of The Riot on their phones, neighbors of Venoa Cove cheered for The Riot. There were cups on the curb, plates upside down on the pavement, and empty lawn chairs in the driveways. Asian Brenda sat on

Haywood's shoulders screaming in excitement. Latina Selena was trying to teach Big Ant how to salsa to alternative rock 'n roll. Blake stood in the back of the crowd behind a tripod recording Becca on video camera. The Yearning Man was wearing a suit in boots with paint spots on them and finger whistled after each performance, yearning to hear more.

Blake thought, "Who is that guy?"

Through the lens, Blake saw Harry following behind Becca after their performance, yearning for her attention. He shrugged his shoulders as they embraced.

He thought, "She's just caught up in the moment."

On the microphone, Harry announced, "Now, it's time to vote!"

Neighbors of Venoa Cove passed around a plastic jar placing a piece of paper with their preference on it inside. The Bass Boys gathered by the coolers. Asian Brenda was pouring juice down Haywood's throat. Latina Selena held a cold soda can on Big Ant's head to keep him cool. Messy Molly and Fish were trying to kiss with ice cubes in their mouth while Blake tried keeping Becca's attention.

"You yearn to sing, don't you?" asked The Yearning Man, approaching them.

"Seriously, I do."

Meanwhile, Harry was announcing the winner.

"And the winner is by one vote... The Riot!"

Becca's band mates rushed to congratulate her as The Yearning Man was adjusting his tie.

Harry hugged Becca saying, "You were so great!"

"Excuse me, but I would like to offer you teens management."

Bran said, "No, thanks, dude."

The Yearning Man said, "I'll work for free."

"Why would you do that?" asked Harry.

"I've always yearned to work in the music business."

"You got the job," said Becca.

Harry said, "She's got the voice. She makes the call."

"I guess I'm going downtown," said The Yearning Man, shaking Becca's hand.

Story 7
What Happens Downtown

Part 1: Sell

The Makeup Misses did makeup for female festival goers on Rosemary's dollar. While the tattoo artist waved people down for face painting beside them, Gentleman Craig sold home decor across from their tables. Lily sold bouquets to people that Lady of Red brought to her wearing the same wig as a form of flattery to her friend. Uncle Moe sat at his table under a tarp surrounded by paintings and tapped his toes as The Riot performed. Neglected Nikki came with Greta and Gary, wearing a mask to pass out toys to kids as the couple sold costume jewelry out their car. Pretty Patty sold her clothes with her mother while her former friend Jessica taught young boys and girls how to flip. As guests greeted Graves, who roamed with his new robot, The Bass Boys stood by Fish's car listening to their own music always with the bass above treble and an open trunk.

"Is he selling that thing? Because I got dibs," said Haywood.

While yo-yoing, he said, "Chicks dig robots, man."

"No, chicks dig smart guys," said Blake, "so I would make it do my homework."

Fish said, "Homework? How about disarming the security system at Venoa Beach Bank, and then unlocking the safe?"

"Then, maybe we could keep the store running," said Haywood, closing the trunk to sit on it.

Blake said, "We can still keep it open. All we need is an investor."

"And where are we going to find one? At orientation?" asked Fish.

"Our parents think we should focus on our schoolwork."

"Face it, man. Pickney's selling the house and the lease with it."

"At least she said we could come visit her in the city," said Fish.

"That's it! We'll go to the city to find an investor."

"Forget about it, Blake."

"Then, we have to get that lease from Pickney," he said.

Haywood said, "Just tell her we found an investor to buy us some time."

Blake was calling her on the phone when he thought, "Please, pick up."

Pickney answered in the middle of the crowd with Tucker at her knee tugging on her trousers. Neglected Nikki rushed to his side with a bag of toys that she held open for him to handpick his favorites. Tucker took too many before Pickney offered to pay. When Neglected Nikki refused her reward, Pickney put a discount coupon for her dance class in the bag while planning to meet with The Bass Boys' supposed investor. Blake told her the man was on vacation and was scheduled to return to Venoa Beach when school started. When they hung up, The Bass Boys opened The Music Man to festival goers, hoping one saw the sign on the door and inquired about investing in the business.

Part 2: Signs

Members of Gifts Church wore matching t-shirts to help promote Preacher Paul's worship concert. As The Riot continued to rock, they passed out fliers to festival goers who were still sweating from dancing to the last song. Danny's parents were among those eager to support Preacher Paul, seeing him as a positive influence on their son.

"My son is going through a tough time," Danny's mother told him.

"He knew that teenage girl who was murdered, didn't he?"

"They were dating."

He said, "It's a sign from God that he should change his life."

"Well, he's always at church."

"But is he investing his time into reading?" he said as his eyes followed Woman Supreme. She was twitching beside Mayor Mark who was carrying a shotgun on a sling around his shoulder. He and The Barrel were selling pellet guns with a free training on how to use them.

Danny appeared with one and said, "Mom, I need fifty bucks."

"Did you speak to your pastor?" she asked.

"I'm mourning, so I have a right to be rude."

Preacher Paul said, "You know, Danny, that with death comes new life."

He asked, "If Cindy's death was a sign, no one can determine what it means for my life but me."

"God wants you to accept Him."

"He has too many rules!" He shouted at the sky, "Let the people be free!"

"God can stop your hurting."

As Danny was walking away, he yelled, "Maybe a reality check can stop your preaching!"

Meanwhile, Fish and Haywood were breaking outside.

Fish asked, "Isn't that the other bang buster?" pointing towards Nakeela's Bar.

He exhaled smoke. "The one we saw at the mall?"

"No, the other one."

Part 3: Exhale

Festival goers crowded the bar making Nakeela unable to recognize who was underage. The two Bass Boys walked in and went straight to the pool table, reaching for sticks before reserving their right to play the next game. They watched the other bang buster as he was downing doubles of dark liquor at the bar, blended in after growing a beard. He slapped fives with male strangers who saw his attempts to seduce women over glasses of wine. After being rejected, he would howl as they walked away. While he was smoking a cigarette outside with Nakeela, Fish watched him through the window as Haywood lined his stick distracted by the game. As people left the bar as The Festival was ending, the two Bass Boys forfeited to begin furthering their plan.

Fish approached the bar saying, "Water, please," as he sat beside the bang buster.

Haywood appeared and said, "Not for him, but for *this* guy with the cool beard."

"What are you two doing in here?" he asked. "Shouldn't you be out slashing tires on someone's car they paid good money for?"

Haywood said, "We didn't slash your tires. We slashed Bobby's."

"Do you think Bobby would try to sober you up right now," asked Fish, "or get you more drunk to hit on women hoping to score?"

"I can't score either way," he said. "At least when I'm drunk, I think I can."

"You're a virgin?" asked Haywood.

"You've been holding a lot in. You have to go for younger girls if you want to finally exhale."

"I want my first time to be amazing," he said.

"And I know an amazing girl."

The bartender asked, "Another one, Howey?"

"Nah, he's good," said Haywood.

"Tip, then?"

Fish said, "Name your price."

Part 4: Price

Jeffery's Kitchen was crowded.

"I think the afterlife is going to be amazing!" Messy Molly exclaimed with a mouthful.

"Then, why doesn't anyone want to die?" asked Howey.

"Because life is amazing, too!" and she put her straw in his cup and told him to sip with her.

He did it and said, "Everybody doesn't live an amazing life."

"But they can!" and she excused herself to the bathroom.

Angel appeared at the table in front of him dressed in all black and waving his finger as the violins played from a radio app on his phone. The waitress brought him an open longneck that he guzzled down before howling. When Howey squinted at him, he winked.

"Do you know me?" asked Howey.

"There's a price to knowing who we are, si?"

"And what's that?"

"Loneliness could be the cost."

He said, "I have two guys that I hang out with."

"There's a price to our associations, si?"

"Venoans don't fear consequences."

"Then, you shouldn't fear death," he said as Messy Molly returned to the table with her hair wet.

"Boys like my hair wavy like this," she said.

"You take my breath away."

"And speaking of heavy breathing, are you ready for me?"

Part 5: Breathe

Messy Molly held onto Howey's arm as they walked down First Street, cutting through the side roads as foot traffic remained steady. She asked him what his best memory of Venoa Beach High was. When he told her that it was graduating, she asked him what his best memory of his entire life was.

He said, "This is."

"Aw," said Messy Molly. "See, all you had to do to get an amazing girl was to be sweet, but real."

"May I?"

"Yes," and they kissed.

"Fish said we could use the store," said Howey.

"Breathe," she told him. "He gave me the key, remember?" and they walked towards The Music Man.

Angel followed behind them singing, *"See you on the other side where you won't have to hide behind tu boys, tu booze, tu beard."*

Meanwhile, The Bass Boys were inside with the lights out.

"Here they come," said Blake, as Messy Molly opened the door. When she turned on the lights, The Bass Boys stood in gas masks.

"What's happening?" asked Howey, as Messy Molly locked the doors.

Fish gave her a gas mask and told him, "Just breathe," as carbon monoxide came through the vent killing him.

Part 6: Masks

People packed Gifts Church from the alter to the back row where cameras were rolling. They lifted their hands as First Lady led them in song sweating behind her veil. Among the people appearing to worship were Danny's parents with their son sitting beside them bored. He skimmed through scripture, ripping out the pages and balling them up to toss at people. After singing the last song, Preacher Paul took to the pulpit dressed down in denim. He opened his Bible and began reading before sharing his message.

Meanwhile, Danny was drinking outside.

He thought, "There's no freedom in religion," and tossed the empty longneck in the bushes.

He pulled out a shotgun that he hid under his mother's clothes in the trunk and stormed inside.

He started shooting and shouted, "Why are you all running?! Today, you're going to Heaven!"

"What are you doing, Danny?!" asked Preacher Paul.

"Removing the masks of the religious!"

"You're ruining your life!"

He shouted, "Who can live up to the Lord's way?!" as tears were flowing.

"Nobody's perfect, Danny!"

"Not even the Lord?!" he asked, aiming at Preacher Paul.

"Haven't you read the story?!"

"That's exactly what it is! A tale! Stop telling people these Bible stories as if they really happened!"

"It's my job!"

He aimed at him and said, "Well, you're fired!" before shooting him dead.

Then, Danny killed himself.

Part 7: Fired

Cathleen was posting information about the memorial following the shooting on the library's bulletin board when The Yearning Man walked in. Unable to find the books he was looking for, as he was brushing his goatee, he followed her to the circulation desk, picking his teeth with a toothpick. The Yearning Man leaned on the counter, smiling at the little librarian as she waited for him to say something.

"I yearn for a smart woman."

"What makes you think I'm smart?"

"Because you surround yourself with books," he said.

"That doesn't mean that I've read them all."

"Well, then," he brushed his goatee, "how about you help me pick some out that you haven't read, so you can read them to me over a cup of coffee?"

"What types of books are you looking for?"

"Business," he said.

"Follow me," and he did.

The Yearning Man continued to flirt with Cathleen as they walked by people sitting in the aisles reading. When he put her arm around her and started to sing, she blushed, begging to talk business to avoid drawing attention to themselves.

"So, do you own a business?" asked Cathleen.

"Not yet," said The Yearning Man.

"Well, what do you do?"

"I yearn."

She said, "I mean for a living."

"Nothing, I was fired for being insubordinate."

"So, how are you going to pay for coffee?"

"I've saved so much money, darling, that I can buy a coffee shop after I open my studio that musicians will yearn to record in."

Part 8: Save

The Bass Boys were in line waiting to talk to Tall Tom, who was detained after paying back the bank.

"He still has to do time, man."

Fish said, "Let's ask him when he's going to turn himself in."

"Maybe we can visit him," said Haywood.

"Guys," said Blake, "we're here to open an account for plan B."

"What's plan B again?" asked Fish.

"We fix up my stepdad's trawler and rent it out."

"The bass boat," said Haywood.

"Chicks dig sailors, man."

"No, chicks dig the beach," Blake said, as they went outside following the bank's safety protocol.

Among those outside was Angel, who was doing push-ups with his eyes on Haywood, who was doing karate movements with his hands.

Gentleman Craig appeared counting cash from selling out at The Festival. The neighbor of Venoa Gardens approached the boys, assuming they were older.

"Excuse me, sirs," he said, "but I'm guessing one of you know a smart girl who would love to dance at my club."

"A night club? There's no flowers in there," said Fish.

"Yea, flowers only," said Haywood.

"Well, you can't save them all," said Gentleman Craig, as they walked back inside.

Tall Tom stood behind the glass typing when The Bass Boys approached the counter. They each took a piece of candy from a dish before smiling at the teller to loosen his guard. When Tall Tom smiled back, Blake pulled out a fake social security card with a fake ID and frowned like the man in the photo.

"Jake, is it?" he asked.

"In the flesh," said Blake.

"You've for sure lost weight."

"Low carb diet."

He looked at the rest of them and said, "Are they eating healthy as well?"

"For sure," he said. "Want to see their IDs?"

"Not for sure," said Tall Tom, "unless they have an account with us, too."

"None of us have an account. That's why we're here."

"Well, there are for sure some papers you will need to sign," walking them to his desk.

"How much time did they give you, man?"

"That is for sure none of your business," he said.

Blake sat and said, "Just show me where to sign."

After sitting himself, he asked, "Savings or checking?"

"Savings," he said.

Blake filled out the paperwork smiling at Tall Tom after each signature. When he asked him what kind of music he listened to, the teller told him country and started singing with twang. Blake sang along as The Yearning Man walked in.

Fish said, "Maybe he can save The Music Man."

Part 9: The Music Man

The Bass Boys waited outside the bank for The Yearning Man after Blake opened an account. They made a plan to lure him to The Music Man with an offer to promote The Riot's first album. When he walked out singing, Fish danced.

"You know, I yearn to learn how to dance like that."

"I can teach you," said Fish.

"Yea, at The Music Man," said Haywood.

"Who's the music man?" he asked, trying to mimic Fish's moves.

"The old man, man."

"I yearn to meet him."

Blake said, "He's dead, but we're still here. We're The Bass Boys."

"The Music Man is actually a store," said Fish.

"We work there, man."

He scratched his goatee saying, "The Bass Boys, huh?"

Haywood said, "And we love music like you do."

"Yea, imagine The Riot posters all over our store," said Blake.

"And their music playing on our loudspeaker," said Fish.

The Yearning Man pondered for a moment before exclaiming, "Take me there!" and they did.

*

With his eyes wide, The Yearning Man browsed CDs and searched the aisles. He sampled songs still mimicking Fish's moves before walking to the back and banging Man's drums singing. He went outside to take a picture of the sign and came back in to pose with the boys who were squinting at his delight.

He stood behind the counter and yelled, "I'll take it!"

Haywood cheered.

"Well, thanks for buying," said Fish, "because we would've been out a job."

The Yearning Man asked, "Who said you still work here?"

"What do you mean?" asked Blake.

"The Riot boys work here now!"

Part 10: Plan B

The newest neighbor of Venoa Cove jotted down Pickney's contact off the sign outside and left. Fish called her right away to tell her not to sell to The Yearning Man and to wait for their supposed investor to return from vacation. When she told them that she would accept the best offer in a hurry to move, Blake reiterated plan B.

The Bass Boys planned to go to by Venoa Beach every day after school until the boat was finished. Blake looked online for a new motor while Big Ant jotted down the prices. Fish drew a picture of what the boat should look like as

Haywood wrote a list of what they needed. They stored Man's karate trophies in the trunk and opened the store to begin pocketing all the cash for their project.

*

During working hours, The Riot boys came in excited about their new job. The Bass Boys just shrugged and pocketed the cash the rockers spent on records before wishing them success. When it was time to close, they recorded themselves on each other's phones doing their handshake as Messy Molly appeared basking in a blue mini dress.

Haywood said, "You look amazing."

"Because she is," said Fish.

With her hands on her hips, she chewed gum, showing off her new foot tattoo in open-toe heels. Her hair was wet and dripping on the thin straps on her shoulders. When she blew a bubble, popping it with her breath, Fish kissed her to remove the gum left on her bottom lip before asking her to slow dance with him to the bass that boomed in his head. The rest of The Bass Boys bowed to their friend and dimmed the lights in the store to further the mood. After the two danced, Fish walked her to his car and opened the door for her to sit. Blake called for a shared ride on his phone as Fish changed clothes, preparing for his date with Messy Molly. The other three Bass Boys rode away before Fish pulled the amazing blond out of the car.

"Will you be my girlfriend?" he asked on one knee.

As The Scooter Crew rode past, she said, "Yes, that was always the plan."

Story 8
The Scooter Crew

Part 1: Extreme

The Bass Boys stood on the cemetery grass drinking beer as traffic persisted on the state road. When they finished one, they opened another, wishing they had more memories to share about Man. Blake watered the flowers as Big Ant began typing a rap song about the old man on a note app on his phone. Fish wrote their names on the tombstone in permanent marker while Haywood was talking to Man as if he were there.

"I'm on the wrestling team," he said.

"And Big Ant and I made the basketball team," said Blake.

Fish said, "I play the bass drum in the marching band."

"And I met a fine Latina, man."

Meanwhile, The Scooter Crew parked their scooters on the other end.

"Where's his helmet?" asked Scott.

Superman sat it by the grave.

"Sweet," said Fat Matt, scarfing a ham sandwich.

Scooter looked over at The Bass Boys and said, "They go to school with us, bro."

"Brothers, that's Molly's boyfriend and his friends," said Superman.

Scott said, "Let's go say hi."

The Scooter Crew revved their engines always screaming in excitement before accelerating. They rode near to each other, keeping speed as they went over humps. As they dodged tombstones with leaning turns, The Bass Boys cheered.

Scott stopped at Man's grave and said, "You guys like that, huh?" removing his helmet.

Fish said, "My girl wasn't lying when she said that you guys were amazing."

"How does it feel to be seniors, man?"

Scooter said, "Half the year is over, bro, and I still don't know my teachers' names."

"He calls them all bro," said Fat Matt, and they all laughed.

"Venoa Extreme is coming up," said Haywood.

"And we're going to kill it," said Scott.

"Sweetly," said Fat Matt.

"Well, see ya' there," as he and his crew revved their engines.

Fish recorded The Scooter Crew on his phone as they rode away.

Part 2: The Scooter Crew

The Scooter Crew sat in detention sharing snacks out of Fat Matt's backpack. The white boy who lost two hundred pounds and was thin as an electric scooter's stem basked in his hunger. With food in his beard, Superman scrolled through his tablet looking at the new menu at Al's Eatery, also as a white boy who ate like an animal. Scooter smacked when he chewed as a tall Black boy with a bearing to stare down competition on the course all while stuffing his face. Scott was the one who led them through the hall on their scooters, earning themselves detention and sat dusting the deck on his own two-wheeler. They were a talented team of tried takers with tremendous taste buds that tested their limits on scooters in an effort to make it pro. When they finished filling their stomachs, they copied each other's homework with sticky fingers, leaving stains on their papers hoping to make their teachers cringe.

"Done, bro?" asked Scooter.

Superman showed him his paper saying, "The chicken scratch of champions, brother."

"Sweet," said Fat Matt.

"Alright, fellas, two hours are up!" and they cheered.

"And we feast."

"*After* we practice," said Scott.

They touched helmets before putting them on and walked their electric scooters out the classroom. They rode down the hall cheering.

Principal Jon laughed before shouting, "That'll be detention again for you degenerates!"

"Sweet!" as the doors slammed shut.

They stopped at Scooter's cargo van in the school parking lot to switch rides. Fat Matt rolled out his red moped on three wheels with a twinkie hanging out his mouth. Superman sat on his blue one playing an air guitar only he could hear. Scott checked the mirrors on his eighty-volt black one that he called Superior as Scooter revved the engine in his cargo van. As the three of them followed him to the skate park in Venoa Park, swerving in lanes as he switched, they cheered with the straps of their helmets slapping them in the face.

Part 3: Switch

Scooter parked with the rest of the crew behind him, shouting out the window to Messy Molly who was playing one-on-one basketball with Fish. The Scooter Crew switched from mopeds to stunt scooters and became serious after the couple left them alone in the park. They tightened the straps on their helmets before putting on pads and rubbed the fur on Wheeler's rabbit's foot for safe landing.

Superman said, "This is for you, brother," looking into the clouds.

Fat Matt tossed a twinkie in the air for Wheeler before they took turns on the ramps. Scooter started with a full whip before spinning his front wheel into a nose pivot. While in the air, the other three cheered as he landed on the deck and continued his routine. Fat Matt was next and began with a back flip off the biggest ramp, ending with a tail whip off the launch. He grabbed the bottom of one sneaker in midair, landing smooth as cream filling in a cool twinkie. Superman tied a bed sheet in a knot around his back and began with a fakie, riding his scooter backwards after turning one hundred eighty degrees in the air. He showed off with a quad whip as Scott shouted out more tricks for him to try. When it was his turn, the other three boys bowed, bestowing their honor upon the best.

Scott tucked Wheeler's rabbit's foot between his knee pad before looking into the clouds, and then closed his eyes for a moment of silence. He started out with a front flip, tucking into a ball. After a soft landing, he went for a triple bar-spin that made Fat Matt spit out his twinkie as Scott rotated the handlebars three hundred sixty degrees three times. He rode at high speed to the quarter ramp and did a whip rewind, catching a tail whip with one foot first and kicking back to the opposite direction and landing. For his finish, he rode to the biggest ramp, picking up speed to perform a double back flip. When he landed, the other three boys ran down the ramp to slap fives with their friend and hoist him up over their shoulders.

"Too sweet."

"Awesome, brother."

"So cool, bro."

Fat Matt said, "And now we feast!"

"We're not done," said Scott. "Again."

"*Sweet.*"

Part 4: Sweet

The Scooter Crew walked inside Al's Eatery with their helmets hanging from their necks. While standing in line, they were picking out which waitress they wanted to serve them.

"She's cute," said Scott.

"Nah, too fat," said Scooter.

"What about her?"

"No, too skinny," said Superman.

Scott saw Neglected Nikki tying her apron and said, "Now, she's sexy."

"That's the one," said Fat Matt, before requesting her.

The hostess said, "She's sweet. She just got over the virus, so you be sweet, too."

Fat Matt said, "Sweet," following her to a table rubbing his stomach. They ordered drinks before she whispered something in the Neglected Nikki's ear and winked at Scott who was watching.

"Hey, boys," said the dropout, "loving our new menu?" as she sat their sweet teas on the table.

"I'm loving your smile," said Scooter.

"I'm loving your hair," said Superman.

"I'm loving your eyes," said Scott.

"And I want to learn how to love *you*," said Fat Matt.

She laughed, "What's a girl going to do with all that love?"

"Free desert?" asked Scooter.

"We'll see," she said.

"Sweet," and she walked away to allow them more time to view the menu.

When she came back with lip gloss on and smelling like lotion, they sat up straight. Scott went first, asking for two orders of hot wings.

Superman ordered two bacon cheeseburgers with sauteed onions added to the sandwich. Scooter cleared his throat before singing his order of two lamb gyros with extra white sauce.

"And I'll have two zinger burgers, two orders of chicken tenders, two fries, and you and me together."

"Sweet," she said.

*

After a male server brought them their food, they stuffed their faces wearing napkins as bibs.

Before they left, Fat Matt approached Neglected Nikki.

"A tip or a talk?" he asked.

"Both?" she blushed.

He said, "Your tip is to think of the dead when you're feeling down. It should remind you to have more fun with your life. The more fun you're having, the less time you have to be depressed."

"What's my talk?

"We'll talk later. Over the phone, perhaps?"

"Okay."

Scott shouted, "We're going to be late for work!"

Part 5: Late

As they waited in the break room for motorcycles to fix, The Scooter Crew watched Wheeler on video doing tricks. Scott's father The Motor was on the other end of the garage working on cars when he heard the boys cheering. With another shop in Major City where he chopped cars with Coach RJ's connections, he drove whatever he wanted with access to the latest models. Venoa Beach High athletes always came by the shop off the state road to salute The Motor. After he and Coach RJ paid for uniforms with money earned from their illegal dealings, they would pay him back with their time.

The Motor was standing outside for air when The Skate Lords from Venoa Oaks appeared.

"You guys don't look like you're friends of my boy."

"We've met you before," said Mike, "at the extreme."

"Venoa Extreme is for real champions like my boy. How many titles have you three won?"

"Well, the extreme combines each sport."

"Is that an excuse, son?"

The Scooter Crew approached them.

"Trading in your skates for a motorcycle, bro?"

The Skate Lords circled them.

"A motorcycle is a lot faster than a scooter," said Mike.

Scott said, "What are you doing here?"

"I just came to wish you guys good luck before it was too late."

"Sure, brother."

"Because my routine is going to ruin Scott's chances to retain."

Fat Matt said, "You know he always kills it on the ramp."

"Like Wheeler killed himself? Life's no fun when you're paralyzed, is it?"

They started fighting.

"Break it up, boys!" exclaimed The Motor and his men who intervened.

"You're lucky we're wearing skates," said Mike and skated away.

Part 6: Buzz

Mayor Mark sat with The Makeup Misses during lunch as Liz was planning Erica's next move as senior class president. Three members of The Scooter Crew were sitting at a table across from them. Fat Matt approached the president after washing down his food with soda.

"Coming to the extreme, ladies?"

"Who's not going?" asked Erica.

"There's literally posters all over school."

Mayor Mark said, "The whole city's buzzing about it."

Meanwhile, The Skate Lords came back to the campus with lunch. While eating in Mike's car, they heard Superman scream in excitement as he drove away on his moped. Mike got out of the car and rushed to Scooter's cargo van and opened the back doors. He stepped inside, searching for Scott's stunt scooter. When he found it, he checked the bolts.

He thought, "I'm getting the buzz this year," and left fast.

Part 7: Fast

Fat Matt and Neglected Nikki were having sex in Scott's bed.

"Too fast," she said, out of breath.

"Okay," breathing heavy.

"Too slow."

"Okay."

"Right there."

"Sweet," he said, before stopping.

When they overheard The Motor singing to his wife, they got dressed. They crept downstairs before rushing out the front door. When she hopped onto Scott's old two-seater scooter, Fat Matt screamed in excitement as he accelerated with her arms around him, heading for the skate park.

Meanwhile, Scooter was practicing.

"You have to go faster if you want to hit that rewind!" Scott shouted.

Scooter did a front flip.

"Nice, brother!"

The Skate Lords appeared.

Scott thought, "What now?"

"Times up, boys," said Mike.

"He's not done," said Scott.

He said, "But you are."

"You're not faster than me."

He laughed, "When was the last time you got laid? You start out slow and steady, remember?"

"Let's go, fellas," said Scott.

"Wait, don't you want to see our routines?"

"We'll see you at the extreme."

Part 8: Routine

Blake and Big Ant were sitting in the bleachers watching Jessica lead the cheerleading squad in a dance routine when Haywood walked in. They did their handshake before the boldest Bass Boy danced to make them laugh. When Big Ant joined him, Blake shook his head smiling as The Scooter Crew interrupted the girls' practice to ensure they bought tickets to Venoa Extreme.

Blake confessed, "Jessica keeps giving me signals."

"So is Becca, man."

"What do you mean?"

He said, "Man, you're not paying attention. Once you see it, I'll show you what I mean."

"She's just stuck in her routine. Homework, rehearsal, and..."

"Harry?" said Haywood.

The Scooter Crew stepped up the bleachers.

"Bro, wait until you guys see Scott's routine tomorrow."

"It's sweet."

"Championship material, brother."

"Where's Fish?" asked Scott.

Blake said, "Breaking the bass drum."

Part 9: Broken

While in a bathroom stall, Scott was watching the first Venoa Extreme event when Wheeler broke his back going for a double back flip. Janitor James walked in.

"Anybody in here?" he asked.

Scott turned off the video on his phone and stood on the toilet as Janitor James started break dancing. He laughed before busting through the stall.

"I didn't know you could dance."

"Break dancing is my passion," putting his hat back on.

"Then, you should pursue it."

As sweat dripped down his dark face, he said, "I got bills to pay."

"It's not about money. It's about the messages you receive while pursuing what you love."

"What *you* love keeps scuffing up my floors. I know who you are, Venoa Extreme Champion."

"Sorry."

"But tell me what you learned."

"I lost my first event, and it cracked me. When Wheeler died, I was completely broken. But we can only see inside our hearts when it's broken, and what you find is what you use to put it back together."

"What did you find?"

"Come to the extreme, and I'll show you my gift."

Meanwhile, The Skate Lords were skipping class.

"Open it," Mike told the two skaters.

They stuck a screwdriver in the back door of Scooter's cargo van.

"Sweet," he said, and stepped inside.

Mike loosened the bolts on Scott's stunt scooter with a ratchet.

Part 10: Stunts

Police surrounded the Convention Center downtown as people pushed and shoved to enter the experience of Venoa Extreme. In an event where skateboards, bikes, roller blades, and scooters were pushed to their structural limits by learners who showed off their limitless use, the risks were everyone's reward. Sneaking beer bong sticks in their backpacks, teenagers stood tipsy waiting for the qualifying run. Rosemary was there with The Makeup Misses. Mandy was cursing out the people blocking her view. The C Students from Venoa Oaks played handheld video games while they waited. While The Scooter Crew was snaking with The Dropouts in the back, The Bass Boys and Messy Molly stood in the front hyping the crowd.

As a skateboarder took to the ramp first after shaking hands with Gentleman Craig at the judges table, everyone cheered louder. When he was finished his run after several kick flips and ollies, ending with a three sixty hard flip, he slapped fives with his crew as a biker took to the ramp.

He wowed the crowd with a three sixty barspin and a seven twenty before ending with a no footer. After the biker saluted the judges who gave him a near perfect score, Mike took to the ramp. He showed off in midair with a couple of three sixties, touching his wheels and landing smooth. After a death drop, he ended with a pump and bowed to the judges.

Scott went for a double backflip first when he landed on his head.

"Bro!" and the rest of The Scooter Crew rushed to aid him.

"He's not moving!" exclaimed Superman.

"His eyes are closed!" shouted Fat Matt.

Medics were checking him when one said, "He's dead."

Story 9
Neighbors Of
Venoa Oaks

Part 1: Scott?

There was a large treehouse neighbors of Venoa Oaks shared to escape the pressure their families put on them to provide. Whether it was children who provided their parents hope, teenagers who gave them inspiration, or parents themselves who provided them support, everyone enjoyed its luxury. As Mike sat inside popping ketamine pills, still in his cap and gown and staring at Scott's picture in the yearbook, Fish came up singing.

"What are you so happy about?"

"Molly," he said.

"Well, the faster she stole your heart, the quicker she'll give it back to you in pieces."

"Is that why you're taking pills, because of a broken heart?"

"No, I killed somebody."

"Why?"

"Because I wanted to be Venoa Extreme Champion."

Fish thought, "Scott?" and then said, "Well, maybe you'll be champion next year. Your class ring is huge!" and he rushed over to see it close up.

"I can punch out a bear with it, right?"

"There's tons of them on the barren road. You should try!"

"It might kill me, but what the hell, I deserve to die." and he slammed the yearbook shut.

Fish said, "Well, gotta' go. Who knows what my aunt is telling my girlfriend right now."

Part 2: Stupid

Fish walked in Aunt Kate's house and grabbed Messy Molly by the hand. As he marched her upstairs, she smiled, assuming he wanted sex. He took her into the bathroom, slammed the door shut, and sat her on the toilet for her undivided attention. While pacing, Fish took off his shirt. To ensure no one could hear, he stuffed it in the crack below the door.

She said, "Please, be something amazing."

"Amazingly *stupid*," he said.

"Tell me."

"Scott's death was no accident."

"How do you know?"

"I don't know for sure, but you're going to find out."

"How?"

"You're going to go to tree house now and tell him how much you hated Scott and see what he says."

"Who's he?"

"He's one of The Skate Lords."

"Okay!"

Meanwhile, The C Students sat in their gaming chairs in separate houses sharing codes over headsets.

Chase said, "This game is stupid."

"We could've made a better one than this," said Chance.

Wyatt said, "The gaming world needs us."

Chase asked, "Do we have enough cash for Video Game Design Camp?"

"No."

"We gotta' do more than a paper route."

Chance said, "Who knows when we'll be able to quit school to make video games."

Part 3: Quit

The C Students sat in the treehouse discussing the details of their first video game over classical music that inspired the boys to think of sophisticated ideas. Chase took notes on his phone, concentrating with his tongue out. He was the organizer who arranged their adventures into the gaming world when they were aggravated by school assignments. As Wyatt waved his finger to the music as the most imaginative, pretending to be video game characters all the time, Chance paced back and forth leading the discussion. While the most gregarious with a great following of online gaming friends, he encouraged them to speak up. They were a gracious group of gamers gifted with great hand-to-eye coordination that would choose a video game over a girl unwilling to kiss.

"So, got any names for it?" asked Chance.

Chase said, "Third Letter World."

"Principal Jon, we quit!" exclaimed Wyatt.

Chance said, "Creating it is going to be easy because we love video games," before overhearing The Lumberjack chopping wood.

Wyatt exclaimed, "Speaking of making things look easy, look at him go!"

"Let's see if he wants some help," and they stepped down.

The Lumberjack was a tall muscular white man who would rather build with men than debate with them as the one responsible for the treehouse. He built it after blackmailing the neighborhood's Board of Directors for money as the member with the most influence. As The Lumberjack wiped his brow with his forearm after every fourth swing, The C Students cheered him on.

"Exercise for a swell man," he said.

They asked, "Can we try!"

"Well, that depends on how swell you boys are?" and he chopped a log and pieces of it flew.

"Do you got three more axes?" Chance asked.

"No, but you boys can take turns with Betty if you promise to treat her like the trophy she is," and he kissed his ax.

The boys took turns chopping wood as The Lumberjack coached them through it.

"Now, don't quit when your arms get tired. It's like life, boys. Keep swinging at it until you're strong enough to take the pain."

"Like this?!" asked Chase.

"That's swell swinging! Now, I have to gather all this wood to see which pieces I can use for my project."

Chance asked, "What are you working on?"

"A log cabin because a mortgage is motivation to live payment free making life that much easier."

"Do you know what would make building it much easier? The three of us helping you!"

"All you have to do is pay for Video Game Design Camp for us!"

"No can do, boys. The Lumberjack works alone."

After they walked away, he went behind the tree house stairs and started digging.

Meanwhile, Sierra was watching from the balcony.

Part 4: Sierra

Sierra wore pigtails and pink as often as Venoans pondered their next bold move. With her socks to her knees in a creased skirt and crew neck, she was avoided by female fashionistas who frolicked in the hall for attention from guys who they gawked at hoping to be given a chance. Sierra spoke with a lisp often about the latest video game, making her lousy at gaining girlfriends. As The Lumberjack counted cash out his suitcase in a hole in the ground, she recorded him on her tablet in the middle of her game to gawk at his muscles.

"Oh. My. Gosh," she whispered.

After reburying the money, The Lumberjack leveled out the dirt and walked away.

Sierra said, "He could curl my whole body!" re-watching the recording. She paused it to wipe her drool before a squirrel appeared. "Are you a boy one or a girl one?" she asked it. "If you're a girl, then check him out!" and she showed it the video. When the squirrel went away, she shouted, "Lesbian!" and came down the stairs.

With her eyes on her tablet after resuming her game, she started her walk home.

*

Her mother opened the door for her and said, "Sierra, muffin, do mind my carpet."

The gamer girl kicked off her sneakers saying, "You need a boyfriend, so you can have something better to do when you get bored than clean."

"And what do you suppose I would be doing with a man?"

"Having sex!"

"Excuse me, young lady."

"Check him out!" she exclaimed, showing her the recording.

"Is that all his money?!"

Sierra said, "Forget the money! Check out those muscles! Don't you want to feel them?"

"Oh, he's too much man for me."

"Not me!" as she stared at him in the video.

"If you want a man like that in your prime, you have to earn better than C's," she said.

"What does my grades have anything to do with it?"

"A man like that needs a smart woman."

"Maybe he can tutor me next year."

"He needs a smart woman because he, perhaps, isn't that smart." Sierra shrugged.

*

While lying in her bed, Sierra edited the video, putting a heart around The Lumberjack. She put her tablet underneath her pillow before placing her headset on and jumping in her gaming chair. She slid across the room on its wheels to her computer and logged in.

She became serious to say, "Alright, Gamer Goblin, prepare to be second best."

Part 5: Gamers

Wyatt was playing an online video game in his bedroom.

"Go left!" exclaimed Chase.

"Now, right!" said Chance.

"Use another weapon, Wyatt!"

"I almost got 'em!" he said.

Chase said, "Let me get a piece of this!" and Wyatt passed him the controller.

"Jump!" said Chance, as a player on-screen intervened.

"Who's Gamer Girl?" asked Wyatt.

"I don't know, but she's good." said Chase.

Over Wyatt's headset, Chance said, "Gamer Girl, reveal yourself."

"Check me out!" said Sierra.

"Where are you from?"

"Venoa Beach!"

*

Part 6: Reveal

Fish and Messy Molly practiced keeping a straight face throughout a staring contest at the kitchen table. When the dancing Bass Boy won after the amazing blond broke into laughter, Aunt Kate joined in, winning after the two teenagers broke into smiles flirting with their eyes. As Messy Molly fed him cookies, he howled like Bobby and The Bang Busters. Aunt Kate shook her head at her nephew as he managed Messy Molly like she was his wife.

With a mouthful, Fish asked, "How much was your fine, Aunt Kate?"

"What fine? Tax fraud?"

"Yea."

"I'm currently under investigation," she said.

"Why did you do it?"

"I'm saving for a yoga studio."

Messy Molly said, "Yoga is amazing."

Aunt Kate said, "Only a healthy Venoan can take the unhealthy risk that's going to help heal the world," and she slammed a condom on the table and told them, "Showers, you two."

"Just in case, huh?" asked Fish on their way upstairs.

*

Messy Molly sat on the bed as her boyfriend undressed.

"Fat Matt called me back," she said.

"Did you tell him?"

"Yea."

"What did he say?"

Messy Molly said, "They have an amazing plan."

Part 7: Plans

Lily sat in a lawn chair, fanning herself with a magazine as Sierra worked in her garden. When the teenager told her to ask The Lumberjack to rebuild her cold frame, Lily pointed to the petunias in the pot that she planned to put in the tree house with his permission. Sierra suggested the succulents go on the stairs and added water to them before putting both flowers in the wheelbarrow.

"Are you taking them now, love?"

"Yes, ma'am," she said.

"Well, he wouldn't say no, would he, love?"

Sierra said, "I'll tell him they're to thank him for his hard work. He can't say no to a question not asked."

"I'll have your cash handy when you get back."

"Great, because I have plans to meet some gamers at the mall for smoothies!"

"Girls?"

"Boys," she said.

Lily said, "When a boy befriends a girl, in most cases, romance is inevitable," and she handed her the magazine to fan her. "Up and down, love, just like that."

"I'm going to be late, Ms. Lily."

The older woman took the magazine and said, "Then, shoo, shoo! You're blocking the sun."

Meanwhile, The C Students took turns playing a handheld video game in the tree house.

"Video Game Design Camp starts in two weeks," said Chase.

"And we have no idea how we're going to get the money," said Wyatt.

"There's always next year, guys."

Wyatt exclaimed, "We got to spend another year at Venoa Beach High?!"

"We couldn't just quit school right away," said Chance.

Chase said, "Yea, we have to learn how to make them first."

As Sierra was coming up the stairs, Wyatt said, "I guess sophomore doesn't sound so bad."

Part 8: Guess

Wyatt asked, "Weren't you in my homeroom?"

"The name's Sierra," putting the petunias against the wall.

"I'm Wyatt, and that's Chance and Chase."

While concentrating on the game with his tongue out, Chase said, "Nice to meet you."

"It's time to go, guys," said Chance.

"Where are you guys going?"

"To the mall to meet some gamer chick," said Chase.

"Gamer Girl?" as she followed them down the stairs.

"Yea, how did you know?"

"Guess," she said.

"You're Gamer Girl?" they asked. When she nodded, the boys praised her for her game play begging for tips. In the middle of talking, Sierra stopped to stare at The Lumberjack, who was carrying a tree trunk over his shoulder. Chance reminded her that she was among boys. When Chase showed his muscle, comparing himself to The Lumberjack, Sierra insisted the boys see him close up to inspire them to get fit. Chance told her they'd rather exercise their minds learning how to make video games instead. Chase unfolded a piece of paper out his pocket and put it in her face to promote their progress.

"Third Letter World," she read aloud.

"Cool, huh?" said Wyatt.

"Let me guess, an adventure?

"With zombies, criminals, and viscous animals!"

Chance said, "We were going to go to Video Game Design Camp, but we don't have the cash this summer."

Sierra pondered before saying, "If I got you guys the cash, can I come to?!"

"We'll do you one better," and the boys whispered to each other.

Chance said, "Tell us, Sierra, how many Cs did you get this past school year?"

"Tons!" she exclaimed.

"Then, welcome to The C Students."

"How about Sierra and The C Students?"

Chase said, "Even better."

Meanwhile, Aunt Kate was arrested at her home.

Fish said, "Don't worry. We'll bail you out."

Messy Molly asked, "Where are we going to get money from?"

"Your guess is as good as mine."

Part 9: Millionaires

Sierra parked Lily's wheelbarrow full of trowels deep in the woods. While waiting for her boys to arrive, she watched the recorded video of The Lumberjack to ensure she knew the exact spot to dig. She moved closer to the tree house after hearing The C Students walking.

She whispered, "*Boys*," and they scurried over.

Sierra put eye black under their eyes, claiming they were at war for their future. When she showed them the spot, all four of them started digging with their hands first, getting as dirty as they assumed the money was. When they uncovered the suitcase, Wyatt held a trash bag open while Chase held another. Sierra and Chance counted the cash before tossing stacks of it inside them.

"That's one hundred thousand so far," said Chance.

"I counted fifty thousand in mine."

Meanwhile, Fish was speeding in circles around the neighborhood with Messy Molly cheering him on in the front seat.

"Let's do it in the tree house!"

"Sex?!" she asked.

"Yea!"

"That would be amazing!" and he parked.

*

Fish was chasing her through the woods.

"Wait!"

Sierra and The C Students were still counting.

"What?" asked Fish.

"Who are they?"

"*Millionaires*. Do you see all that money?!"

"But is it theirs?" she asked.

"Let's ask them!" and they walked up to them, startling the freshmen.

Fish said, "You know, you guys could go to Venoa Beach Juvenile Jail for this."

"Venoans don't fear consequences," Chance said.

"How much do you want?" asked Sierra.

"Enough to bail my aunt of jail."

Sierra said, "Give them half."

"We're rich!" exclaimed the couple.

Story 10
What Happens
In Venoa Beach
Juvenile Jail

Part 1: Bleed

Four boys were fighting.

"Code blue!" yelled Officer Rob over a two-way radio.

Haywood stood on the table to see over the raging crowd that encouraged the boys to bleed for their respect. As the unit filled with officers, more fights broke out, leaving the boldest Bass Boy with no room to retreat to his cell door. Bodies were on the floor covering bloody footprints left by tough boys who teamed up to trample on a bystander. Officers forced to use their fists shed blood as Superintendent Ernie rushed in with a bag of restraints. With the dicey delinquents in handcuffs after being brought down to the floor by force, the crowd scattered to their cells where they beat on the doors begging to see more bloodshed.

"You're bleeding," Haywood told his cellmate Quin.

With a feminine tone, he said, "I'm used to it," and snorted blood.

"Used to getting punched for no reason?"

"No, used to being singled out because I'm a gay white boy."

"Do you want to be gay?"

Quin said, "It's not about what I want. It's about who God made me."

Haywood scratched his head asking, "But do you know who you are in your entirety?"

"I know I'm gay," he said, crossing his legs.

"You're just sensitive," said Haywood.

Quin said, "I become less and less sensitive each time I bleed for being gay."

"Well," he sat up in his bunk, "you won't bleed in here as long as Hero is around to protect you."

"Who's Hero?"

"Me," and they shook hands.

Quin opened up to Haywood as the boldest Bass Boy encouraged him to be himself. The feminine male found a friend in him being forthcoming. He was charged with grand theft after taking a school bus on a joy ride while babysitting. When

Haywood told him that he spray painted The Music Man window before The Yearning Man caught him on the new cameras outside, he basked in his boldness assuming he was bolder.

"What did you write on it?" asked Quin.

"The Bass Boys."

Part 2: Boys

In the cafeteria, the delinquents sat in silence scheming on each other's meal. While they wanted more food, Officer Rob wanted more time with Princess, who served the boys, hiding her empathy for them. She was fair-skinned with long black hair she tied into a bun to fit under a hairnet. The boys waited all day to see her, licking their lips eager for her to smile for them. After working with Superintendent Ernie, who was housing wanted criminals in exchange for cold hard cash they used to establish a college fund for delinquents, she planned to become a probation officer for girls troubled like the ones she fed.

"Write it down."

"My number?"

"Your address," Officer Rob flirted.

She asked, "Are we fraternizing?"

"Venoans don't fear consequences," as the boys began to whisper.

"That doesn't mean we can't take our jobs seriously."

"If money makes you get serious, then love should make you get determined like I am to spend quality time with you," he said as the boys laughed out loud. "Hey, what's funny about being locked up?"

"This meatloaf kills," said Graves.

"You're not going to die from eating meatloaf."

Haywood said, "Yea, especially when she made it, right, officer?"

"Watch it, son," he said.

"But no, officer," the dropout explained, "when I say kills, I mean it as something good."

Curiosity said, "There's nothing good about killing. Keep saying it, and somebody's going to kill *you*."

"No talking," said Officer Rob.

Haywood whispered to Quin, "Are you okay?" as the queer sat with his eyes closed.

"I'm writing in my head."

"A story?"

"A love letter," he said, as they dumped their trays.

"You have a boyfriend?"

"Not yet," he said.

All the boys eyed Princess as they got in line to leave.

Part 3: Kills

Haywood sat behind Quin as the queer finished writing the last line of a love letter while Mr. Lucas shared his life's lessons. Half the class was nodding off when Officer Rob started to roam the rows to check their notes. Curiosity wrote a song called Kills, Graves made a new blueprint for The Crazy Cupid Machine, and the rest wrote nothing but their nicknames over and over.

"Any questions?"

Haywood said, "I heard that your college degree was a fake."

"Indeed, I graduated college," said Mr. Lucas, pacing, "but then I had a degree made with a more prestigious school name on it to appear smarter."

"Why?"

The teacher explained, "So, that my children would think they're smart, thus applying themselves to actually become smart."

"Being smart kills," said Graves.

"Curiosity does, too," said the conscious rapper.

Part 4: Whispers

Some of the boys gathered at the goal to pick teams for a game of basketball in the sun surrounded by barbed wire fences. Others walked around seeking connections to pass the time. Quin sat while Haywood was exercising on the side, coaching Graves through a series of sit ups. When the dropout gave up, struggling to keep up as the boldest Bass Boy showed off his brute strength, Haywood suggested he sit to hide his weaknesses from the dicey delinquents.

"What are you in here for anyway?" he said as the boys on the court were whispering.

Graves said, "I stole a transmitter for a race car out the box in the mall."

"Building another robot?"

"No, something else," he said.

"Hey, I've got an idea that can make you a lot of money."

"Enough to move out of Venoa?"

"Maybe," said Haywood. "My friend Fish just got rich."

"What's the idea?"

"The Bass Bot," he said.

One of the boys yelled, "We need two more!"

Curiosity shouted, "They want to play!"

"Us?" said Graves, looking at Haywood.

"Okay!" said the boldest Bass Boy.

*

After running up and down the concrete scoring the ball a few times, they singled out Haywood who struggled to get open. Graves got the ball and passed it to him as the defense eased off him. Haywood penetrated before being surrounded by two big boys who fouled him to the ground. The boldest Bass Boy stood to his feet and charged at one, wrestling him off his feet. The rest of the boys jumped in.

They assumed, "You like fagots!" stomping him. Graves pushed and shoved to his rescue.

"Code blue!"

Part 5: Blue

After time in confinement, Haywood was last to use the phone, calling Asian Brenda who just moved into Venoa Preserve from Venoa Farms. They played a game, asking each other random questions before she told him he was changing her mind. After getting to know Haywood, Asian Brenda felt brave enough to begin calling the boldest Bass Boy her boyfriend after a broken heart. She bolted out the back door to blurt it to the blue sky before hanging up.

Officer Rob thought, "Strong kid," locking Haywood in his cell.

"Who did you call?" asked Quin.

"My new girlfriend, I guess," said Haywood, lying on his back.

He crossed his legs saying, "You don't seem happy about it."

"Well, there's one condition to starting a relationship with her."

"And what's that?"

Haywood said, "We have to be together for a year before we have sex."

"She wants to see if you can be loyal. You should've told her that your jumper was blue, the color of trust."

"Sex is something you feel before you do it! When you want it and can have it, you can't control that emotion."

"You can't wait that long."

"No," fumed Haywood, "and if she can, that worries me."

"When did you meet her?"

"Last summer!"

"And she hasn't given you any yet?" asked Quin, biting his lip at Haywood who was unaware.

Part 6: Unaware

With the boys out of their cells, roaming the unit bored with their routine, Officer Rob observed them while posted with one foot on the door and the logbook in his hand. When he opened it to record their movement, Curiosity formed a gun with his hand, aiming at Graves who was unaware while doing pushups with Haywood.

"Who's his cellmate?" he whispered to somebody standing next to him.

"Suspect," he said. "He lives in the apartments on the state road."

"What's he locked up for?"

"Murder."

Curiosity said, "Introduce me," and he did.

Suspect was clean cut with a calm disposition to cover the dirty deeds that he dared to do at the cost of his own freedom. With his short sleeves rolled up to reveal his muscle definition that he was revered for, he slapped fives with Curiosity, who complimented his slip-on shoes. Suspect cleaned them every night with a toothbrush and bubbling paste. He cuffed his pants for a neater look before scowling at his cellmate who was still unaware.

"Killing is not cool," said Curiosity.

"But it can be necessary."

Part 7: Killer

The boys were watching a movie when Curiosity tapped Graves on the shoulder.

"Let me talk to you," he said, and they stood aside.

"What's up, killer?"

"Are you a true Venoan?"

"Are you?" said Graves.

"True Venoans don't fear death."

"Death is always a consequence, a lurking one."

"Thank you for inspiring me."

Graves said, "Not enough gets done without inspiration."

The boys scattered to their cells as the movie was ending, leaving Haywood, the only one clapping for an encore. Once the doors were secured, the lights went out. Graves was fast asleep when Suspect put a pillow over his face, pressing down as the dropout kicked and swung his arms for air.

"Curiosity kills," said Suspect.

Part 8: Air

Haywood stood in his seat as the rest of The Bass Boys walked in for visitation wearing matching outfits. They did their handshake before sitting to fill him in on the progress they made with the trawler that Blake said looked about new. When Big Ant told him his plans to ask out Latina Selena after they were finished with it, he suggested they steer to a place on the water to unwind with wine. The three of them saluted him after hearing about his new relationship with Asian Brenda, who Jessica said made a shirt that read, "Hero" according to Fish.

"I don't believe her," said Haywood.

"Then, why did you agree to date her?" asked Blake.

"Because she's like air to me."

Fish blew a bubble and asked, "What did she tell you?"

"No sex for a year."

"That's crazy, man."

"She'll change her mind," said Blake.

Fish said, "And if she doesn't, you change it for her."

"How?"

Quin stood from his seat after visiting with family.

"That's time!" exclaimed Superintendent Ernie.

Haywood said, "Oh, remember that kid with the robot?"

"Yea," they said.

"He's dead."

Quin controlled his attraction to Haywood as they were put in restraints. As they walked back on the unit, the boys were waiting their turn for phone calls before dinner. When Haywood refused his privilege, Quin sized him up as seconds.

Part 9: Seconds

Quin was next to be served.

"Ketchup, please," he told Princess.

"Is that enough?"

"More," said Quin. "It's for my hot dog. He's over there."

Princess piled his tray with packets smiling and asked, "Midnight snack?"

"Seconds," he said and winked, walking away with his head high.

Part 10: Touch

Haywood was pacing in his cell when the lights went out.

"Brenda doesn't burn with desire for me."

"But I know who does."

"Who?"

"Touch me," and he placed Haywood's hand on his face.

The boldest Bass Boy said, "You're sweating."

"You make me hot."

Haywood took off his jumper and said, "So, then touch it," and Quin grabbed him by the crotch.

"How does it taste?"

"You tell me." And he told him throughout the night with ketchup on his mouth.

Story 11
Neighbors Of
Venoa Preserve

Part 1: Destiny

After snatching clothes off the hangers in her closet, tossing them in a pile so high that she could lay in it, Jessica tried sitting on a suitcase full of shoes in an attempt to close it. When one of her heels made a hole on the side, she screamed in frustration, startling her mother who came to her door to advise her. She told her they could take two trips to campus if she was determined to take everything with her.

"Really, mom?"

"Well, I think you should leave some of your things here."

Jessica said, "I'm never coming back."

"And miss your family and friends?"

"There's one person that could make me come back."

"Your mother, of course."

"No offense, mom, you're a bore," she said.

"*Becca* then," she assumed, "because I know for sure it's a woman because we stick together."

Jessica said, "Close, but you don't know him."

"Him? You would let a boy come between you and Becca?"

"He didn't do anything," she said. "It's destiny."

"And does destiny have a name?"

She jumped in the pile and said, "Precious."

Part 2: Piles

Precious stood outside waving a flag at moving cars and walkers, welcoming them to her home where she ran her fortune telling business. She wore a teal turban with a ruby in the center that she believed would attract lovers willing to spend to keep their spark. Standing barefoot in a toga, she chanted syllabic melodies to serenade the squirrels, hoping to seduce somebody into a sell. When Asian Brenda squeezed her bike breaks while being chased by Haywood on his own fifteen speed, Precious ran into the road to wipe the tire marks with her foot.

"Yay! A real live psychic!"

Haywood asked, "Doesn't that hurt?"

"I have strong feet," said Precious, wiping her toes.

"Can we do a reading, Hero, please, please, please?!" begged Asian Brenda.

"I guess so," he said.

"Yay!"

Precious said, "I'll make two piles from several decks. It will be up to you to choose which is for whom."

"Me or her?"

"Both," she said, "and what you choose will be," as she walked across her lawn to her front door. Asian Brenda scurried behind her as Haywood smoked a cigarette that he said was his last. Coach Brock urged him to quit before senior year with plans to prep him as champion. He put his cigarette out and did lunges the whole way to the front door. When he got inside, Asian Brenda looked at him with concern.

"What's wrong?"

Precious said, "I believe you should sit," as she shuffled.

Asian Brenda held onto Haywood with her head on his shoulder as the boldest Bass Boy braced himself. Precious made the first pile with her eyes closed and started stacking the others, staring at the two teenagers. When she finished, she began meditating, breathing in and exhaling onto the piles.

"How much did you pay her?" whispered Haywood.

Precious overheard and said, "We all pay a price, though money is not always the cost."

"May we pick our pile?" asked Asian Brenda.

"You may pick yours," she said.

"Yay!" and she chose.

Precious turned the cards over saying, "I see that pain has caused you to become selfish. You're protecting your heart when it should be shared. You've learned to respect yourself. However, you must learn to respect other people's feelings by being interested in what they feel, or by discerning what they feel to avoid sabotaging what could be a lasting connection."

"Will Hero and I last?"

"Every battle is a hero's battle. This makes their lives more at risk than a true Venoan who doesn't fear the consequence of death."

Haywood asked, "Am I going to die?"

Precious laughed and said, "We all will, my sweet, but not before we bare our souls," staring back at the cards.

"What else do you see?" asked Asian Brenda.

"More pain," she said.

Haywood blurted, "That's enough of this," grabbing his girlfriend by the hand and walking her out.

Part 3: Girlfriends

Haywood hopped back on his bike with Asian Brenda in his ear, begging to go back in to finish her reading.

As Jessica drove past waving at them with Becca belting in the front seat, the boldest Bass Boy thought, "*Girls*," before riding off.

Becca stepped out in style after Jessica parked along the curb. As the performer posed in the mirror tint on the passenger side window, Jessica fixed her friend's hair. With her open toe heels wrapped around her leg, Becca walked up the driveway with Jessica behind her fanning her with her hand. Blake was on his way from The Motor's shop with Becca's car as the couple planned a getaway to Major City before his senior year.

Jessica said, "Let me show you what the flier looks like so far," as they went upstairs to her room.

"You're seriously a legend for throwing these two parties."

"You should really thank Erica. It's her dad that has the yacht."

"The Makeup Misses," Becca mocked them.

"And you know wherever The Makeup Misses are, there are older guys," said Jessica, logging into her computer.

"And Blake will never know. It's graduates only, remember?"

"What about Harry, girlfriend?"

Becca gulped and said, "Just show me the flier."

The doorbell rang.

Jessica exclaimed, "That's him!" jumping out her chair.

"Where are you going?"

While doing her makeup in the bathroom, she yelled, "I have to pee!"

Becca thought, "Blake's making you pee yourself?"

Part 4: Pissed

Jessica opened the front door.

"It's too bad I'm not taking *you* out," said Blake, with an open beer can.

"What do you mean?" as Becca was coming downstairs.

"You look good."

"As good as she does?"

Blake stepped inside as Becca tied her heels on the stairs. When she stood up straight to show herself off, he grabbed her face for a kiss.

Becca pulled away and said, "Have you been drinking?!"

"Don't you yearn for me anymore?"

"Where are my keys?!" and he gave them to her.

She stormed outside as he stumbled on the stairs.

"I have to piss," he said, as Jessica helped him up.

She said, "The bathroom's over here," and walked him to it.

He urinated with the door open.

"Do you want me to close it?" asked Jessica.

"You're such a good friend," he said, zipping his slacks.

"How good?"

"This good," and he grabbed her face.

After a long kiss, she asked, "Make me stay?"

"I can't," he said and left.

Part 5: Kissed

After slamming soggy twenties on the table, Jessica exclaimed, "He kissed me!" as Precious shuffled a pile of cards.

"Why are they wet?"

She said, "Like I am?"

"Aroused, much?"

"It's his fault that I can't stop thinking about him!"

"No, it is the fault of destiny," as she turned the cards over.

Jessica smiled and said, "Well, what do they say?"

"Pain may postpone your pleasure."

Asian Brenda appeared saying, "The door was open."

Jessica left.

Precious stood from the table and scurried over to Asian Brenda with open arms. After a long embrace, Precious told her to walk the trail of quartz crystals leading to the table.

Asian Brenda asked, "Where were these last time?"

"Waiting to heal."

"But I'm not hurt anymore."

"Healing never stops," as they sat.

With Jessica's cards scattered on the table, Precious meditated. When she opened her eyes, Asian Brenda was holding a card in her hand, squinting at the details in the picture on it.

She turned it upside down and said, "How does someone manage to get three swords in their heart?"

"That what you hold is the three of swords."

"What does it mean?"

"Pain is often foretold in its depiction."

"If I'm holding it," she dropped it, "does that mean Hero's going to cheat on me?"

Precious yawned before saying, "He will not take a liking unto anyone else," as she reshuffled, "though to be kissed can cause an arousal needing to be quenched."

Asian Brenda stared down each card as Precious revealed them.

"They're so pretty!"

"And beautiful will be an experience to come."

"Tell me more!"

Precious said, "It will begin with a message," as she gathered the cards.

"What are you doing?"

"That's all for now," she said, getting up.

"What about pain?!"

Precious told her, "Pain of some sort is inevitable for teenagers who are moving forward in their lives yet haven't lived them yet," as Asian Brenda followed her to the front door.

"One more piece of advice, please?!" the teenager begged.

She held the door open for her and said, "Do not underestimate your kiss," before shutting her out.

Part 6: Shut

Jessica sat at her computer putting the finishing touches on the flier before emailing it to Erica. After hours on the phone, they were sure no one would miss the party on the marina before the one on the yacht. Jessica did a cartwheel to her closet where her brand-new bathing suit hung alone. She tried it on again as Becca began banging on her room door.

Jessica opened it and posed when Becca exclaimed, "This is serious!" and shut the door behind herself.

"It can't be more serious than me in a bikini."

"You do look hot," she said.

"Blake was looking hot the other night."

"Blake is hot, but Harry makes me hotter."

Jessica asked, "You two had sex?!"

"A few times?"

"Shut up! Why didn't you tell me the first time?"

"Because," said Becca, "I didn't get pregnant the first time."

Part 7: Time

Precious was meditating when Haywood appeared at her window after testing the knob on the front door. The light in her home became dark from his shadow blocking the sun. She opened her eyes and turned her head towards the window with a serious face. She signaled for him to go around to the garage before lighting a candle, placing it on the window seal. Haywood was inside when she took off her turban and shook her hair after unwrapping it.

"You're beautiful," he said.

"So is your heart."

"Is now a bad time?"

"Sit," she said, and he did.

"But I don't have any money."

"Money is worthless on the other side," as she shuffled the cards.

Precious pulled one card after the other, turning them over on the table for her to see. After nine cards, she stopped.

"Why nine?" asked Haywood.

"The number of completion."

"What's completed?"

"Your quest to becoming the hero they've called you for so long," as she stared down at the cards.

Haywood said, "No one can out-wrestle me."

"It is your time."

"I knew I was going to be champion senior year!"

"You've always had the heart of a champion."

He jumped to his feet and exclaimed, "I'm going to go tell my girl the good news!" before leaving.

Precious blew the candle out.

Part 8: Blow

Haywood petaled at full speed before stopping in the driveway where he assumed Asian Brenda was asleep in her father's RV. He swung open the door and stepped inside to find her sitting with the unfolded love letter from Quin. With tears flowing, she read it aloud before Haywood snatched it from her. As he tore it to pieces, she punched his shoulders. She tried putting the paper back to together to finish reading it as he paced back and forth.

"You had sex with a boy in jail?!"

"He gave me some head," Haywood admitted.

She turned on the faucet and splashed him saying, "A blow job? Cheater!"

"It was your fault!" as he followed her to the front.

"So, it's my fault that you're gay?!"

He punched the window and said, "I'm not gay. I'm desperate!"

"Desperate for what?!" and she slammed the cabinet.

"Sex, or anything close to it!"

"So, you would've had sex with him if you had a condom?"

"No," he sat her down, "I'm not attracted to boys! I'm attracted to sex, and sex with me involves kissing!"

"So, when we kiss," she batted her slanted eyes, "it makes you want to have sex. Why didn't you just tell me that?"

Haywood said, "Because I want you to want it because you want to, not because I do."

She bit her lip before saying, "I'm going to make sure we don't blow this relationship."

"How?" as she felt his arms.

"By making sure you never feel like you have to do that again," and she kissed him from his cheek to his forehead. Haywood admired her hair with his hands as she batted her slanted eyes at his chest. She kissed around his mouth before biting his lip. Haywood picked her up by her thighs and sat her on the bathroom sink where they kissed with more tongue than they used to talk. With their clothes on the floor and his sneakers still on his feet for leverage, he carried her to the kitchenette where he sat her on the stove.

"I'm sorry, Hero," out of breath.

"I'm sorry, too," while they were having sex with ketchup on their bodies.

Part 9: Sorry

"So, did you tell him?" Jessica asked, after hanging up with Erica.

Becca said, "So he can die?!" and covered her face with a pillow.

"He's not going to die from a broken heart."

"I can just see pieces of it everywhere."

"Hey," she took the pillow from her to look into her eyes, "what if someone was there to pick them up?"

She asked, "What if no one has to because he never knew I was pregnant by another guy?"

"You're being selfish," said Jessica.

"Seriously, best friend?"

"It's either going to be Blake or Harry."

"I seriously can't decide!"

She blurted, "Blake kissed me, sorry!"

"What!" and she hit Jessica with the pillow.

"Now, can you decide?"

"So, you're the one who wants to pick up the pieces!"

"Wouldn't you rather see him with someone you love than some random chick?!"

Meanwhile, The Bass Boys stepped out of Fish's car parked along the curb. As their music blasted, always with the bass above treble, they walked up the driveway with Blake in front.

After he rang the doorbell, Haywood spat. Big Ant stood with his head high as Fish counted cash leftover from The Lumberjack's stash.

Jessica opened the door and said, "Hey, boys."

"Where is she?" asked Haywood.

Fish said, "She's been avoiding him."

"Why, man?" as Becca appeared behind Jessica with her eyes wide.

"Tell him," Jessica told her.

Big Ant passed Blake his phone.

"Don't tell me anything," he said, showing the girls the video recording of Becca on top of Harry.

"Well, you kissed Jessica!"

"I was drunk."

Jessica blurted, "They had sex!"

Fish asked Becca. "Can I be next? I got a twenty," and he tossed the bill in the air.

Blake shook his head and said, "Dragonflies? That was you being emotional. We can't always trust what we feel."

With tears flowing, Becca said, "I'm sorry, seriously!"

Part 10: Serious

Fish drove off with Big Ant in the front seat bobbing his head to the music. Haywood put his face out the back window beside Blake, who was scrolling through photos of bikini models on his phone. Precious flagged them down.

They were all standing outside the car when Fish exclaimed, "You could've gotten yourself killed, lady!"

"Death is no accident."

"Why did you stop us, man?"

"First, you will acknowledge me as the woman I am. Second, it is destiny that has you four standing outside my home."

Blake said, "We don't know anyone named Destiny, so you're wrong."

"I'm as serious as you four are concerning women," she said.

"Guys, she has powers," said Haywood.

"Show me," said Blake, following her inside.

Precious walked them to the living room where they took turns pretending to see things in her crystal ball. After sharing laughs, Big Ant flopped on the sofa beside Blake. Haywood did push-ups while Fish danced. When Precious came in from the kitchen with five snack cakes on a tray with candles, they reached for them, eager for a taste.

"Don't," she said, as they were about to eat.

"Can we at least blow out the candle?" asked Fish.

"No," said Precious.

"Too late," said Haywood.

"Why is there an extra one?" Blake asked. "There's only four of us."

She said, "There is another," with her eyes closed.

"What is she doing, man?"

"Meditating," said Haywood.

She opened her eyes over her crystal ball and said, "Party. Bikinis. Trunks. Booze. Drugs. Dancing. Kissing..."

Fish interrupted, "Wait, we don't do drugs."

Precious said, "Water surrounds you four," and walked away.

"Jessica's throwing a yacht party by Venoa Beach, but it's graduates only," said Blake.

"She'll let us in, man. She likes you."

Haywood said, "Becca needs to see you having fun."

"We should focus on finishing the boat."

Fish said, "I agree," as Precious dealt them each a card. She sat with the rest on the throw rug, shuffling before choosing two cards that she said would reveal a serious message. The Bass Boys each looked at their card confused before she began to explain.

"That what you hold is the emperor," she told Blake. "You're the leader with a positivity that inspires your friends."

"What about mine?" asked Haywood.

"The ace of cups, my sweet, suggests that you are the heart of the four of you."

Fish said, "Mine has a sword."

"And swords represent the mental aspects of being. You are the mind of the bunch."

"Mine looks pretty cool, man."

"That what you hold is the high priestess, a spiritual guide. You are the soul of this support system."

After turning over the two cards, she scowled at her reflection on the television screen. She looked into each of their eyes before smearing her lipstick. The Bass Boys watched her as she bent her earrings and let strands of hair hang from her turban.

Haywood asked, "Are you okay?"

Precious said, "What I'm showing, my sweet, is what the inside of a woman could look like."

"I knew that," Fish said.

"Yea," said Blake, "just tell us what the cards say."

"Don't take women too seriously, even when you intend to be monogamous is the message."

"Why, woman?"

"Because we women are not as innocent as we seem, therefore, have no expectations. Now, eat!"

Story 12
What Happens By
Venoa Beach

Part 1: Heart

Homeless Man Twenty was telling a story when Angel appeared in the crowd with a stethoscope around his neck.

"The end," and people scattered off the pier.

Angel approached him asking, "That is your heart you share, si or no?" and lifted the old man's shirt.

"This is why I stopped going to the doctor."

While listening for his heart, he said, "Nothing there."

Homeless Man Twenty asked, "Where are your credentials?" and put his shirt down.

"Who needs credentials when you have experiences?"

"Experiences don't mean shit if you don't learn from them. What happened to you the last time you talked to strangers, ay?"

"Our souls connect us, making us brothers, si? And as mi hermano, I must give you much needed advice."

"What is it?"

"Kill yourself," and walked away.

Meanwhile, Will was walking on the beach.

He threw a rock in the water saying, "Catch, Graves!" and watched it land on a wave. The dropout took off his shirt, revealing his late friend's name tattooed on his heart. In a masculine stance, he looked in the sky above the water and cried without making any noise.

Part 2: Noise

Surrounding a sculpture made of wood were people dressed down after docking their boats. Uncle Moe was among them taking pictures, disregarding the rules of the art museum that forbid it. Beside him was Neglected Nikki whispering on the phone with Fat Matt. She started laughing out loud to make Will jealous as he walked in still with sand in his crocs.

"Our best friend is in the grave. What's funny about that?"

She ended the call and said, "Hey, I cried for days."

"Well, I still cry," he said.

"Shh," said Uncle Moe. "Do you hear that noise?" he said scurrying over to a painting on the wall. He put his ear to it and said, "It's talking. The colors are so loud. What a joyful noise!" He rushed to another on the wall to interpret it. "This one is a mellow noise, repetitive." Before pulling his nephew and Neglected Nikki with him to the last one, he pretended to tap dance.

"What noise do you hear from this one, Uncle Moe?"

He said, "Sounds like... pain," and took a picture.

Meanwhile, Homeless Man Twenty walked in.

"Excuse me, sir!" said security.

"What is it?"

The Keeper of the art museum said, "You'll need to take a shower before you come in here, please."

"I saved my last dollar to enjoy the finer things before I die of this virus going around, and I get harassed, ay?"

Security said, "You can just come with me," and grabbed him by the arm.

He shouted, "Unhand me!" when Will appeared.

A guest asked, "Is that him making all that noise?"

"You need to take a shower!" The Keeper exclaimed.

As security walked Homeless Man Twenty out, Will thought, "I'm going to give him a blood bath."

Part 3: Dirty

Haywood scrubbed the deck on the starboard side, rapping along to the music playing in the fly bridge area where Blake swept. While wiping the pilothouse windows, Fish danced. Big Ant polished the wood cabin, bobbing his head to the bass that boomed from their wireless speakers.

Angel appeared on the pier and shouted, "How many Venoans have clean hands?!"

"What?!" yelled The Bass Boys.

"Turn down the music!" he exclaimed, and they did.

"Any new tattoos?" Fish asked, stepping onto the pier.

Angel said, "A tattoo should remind you of who you are. I'm a Venoan with dirty hands willing to deceive for the greater good."

"We only deceive when we feel it's necessary!" Blake exclaimed, coming down from the fly bridge.

"But that doesn't rid you of the consequences, mi amigo!"

Haywood stepped off the boat and asked, "What's the worst that could happen?"

"Death," said Angel, and walked away with his head low.

Blake shouted for Big Ant who came out the cabin rubbing his stomach like the rest of them. They walked to Rick's Restaurant with their matching boat shoes untied before finding a table closest to the bar to admire Julianne working behind it. Her brunette hair was crimped past her shoulders and shined brighter after her breaks when she touched it up with spray. While pouring, she smiled wide, making the bad days of male guests better. The Bass Boys gave her compliments to each other until Blake raised his voice for her attention.

"And you're how old?"

He asked, "According to the number of birthdays I've had, or the number of conversations I've had with gorgeous girls like you?"

"Gorgeous?"

"Drop dead," he said.

Fish said, "His ex-girlfriend did him dirty, so the least you could do is give him a drink."

"How dirty?"

"She cheated," said Blake.

"So, you gave up?"

"Wouldn't you?" asked Haywood.

"Well, maybe it's deeper than that," said Julianne, bringing them each a shot.

"What do you mean, man?"

"Maybe there's more to her story."

"So, you're saying that I should find out why she did it?"

Julianne said, "Absolutely."

Part 4: Find

Neglected Nikki found Will in The Shopping Center.

"Look what I have," waving a flier in his face.

"A piece of paper?"

"Read it!"

"I would if you held still," said Will, before she read it aloud. "I thought you wanted me to read it."

"You were taking too long!"

He said, "I swear I don't understand women," shaking his head.

"Did you hear what I said?!"

"There's a party on the marina followed by another one on a yacht starting tomorrow afternoon."

She said, "The two Fat Matt was telling me about."

"Is he serious about you?"

She smiled saying, "Jealous, are you?" as Sierra and The C Students walked out Alvin's Arcade in shades.

Sierra unbuttoned her baseball jersey for air when Will said, "I have to go to the sporting goods store. Find Uncle Moe," and Neglected Nikki nodded before going.

With goggles on after searching the ski section, Will roamed around until he ran into Pretty Patty in uniform. Her hair was dyed dark red and hung over her shoulder in a ponytail. Gloss shined on her lips and smelled sweet.

"Can I help you find something?"

He said, "A heart," removing the googles, "not for me, but never mind. What does a girl like you know about sports?"

"What exactly is a girl like me?" as they walked.

"Well, your nails are done. Can't swing a bat with hands like that."

"What if I don't play softball?" as she played with her ponytail.

"Can't shoot a basketball with those either. You need your fingertips to follow through."

"Well, my boyfriend wrestles."

"That's cool," licking his lips, "but there's nothing like hitting a home run," and he handed her his phone.

She blushed and said, "I can't give you my number."

"But you want to," he said. "Listen, if you can't give me your number, you could at least give me a discount."

"On those," she glanced at the goggles.

"And a *bat*," he said.

Pretty Patty led him to the proper aisle where Will was reminded of pitching for Venoa Beach High's varsity team as a freshman. Before being kicked off the team for poor grades, he struck more people out than there were students on the principal's list. When he dropped out after he and Graves built a voice powered dumbbell that got heavier on demand, assuming it would afford them a city villa, he took his favorite aluminum bat with him. Pretty Patty watched him as he tested several by swinging them with all his strength.

Holding a wooden one, Will thought, "I'm going to find you, old man," tightening his grip as he stared at it.

"Find one you like?"

"Yea," still staring.

"There's two parties starting tomorrow afternoon. Maybe I'll see you there?"

"Maybe."

"And in my bikini, I won't be hard to find," Pretty Patty said and winked.

Part 5: Hard

Uncle Moe left Will asleep on his sailboat after Neglected Nikki begged him to take her back to Venoa Gardens. While she was home preparing for the parties the following day, Will was practicing his swing after awakening at night. Afterwards, he wrote Neglected Nikki's full name on the barrel. He swung a few more times before starting his search for Homeless Man Twenty.

While taking a shared ride to the boardwalk, the driver asked him, "What's with the bat?"

"Baseball fan," he said.

"You could've just worn a cap," as he pulled over.

Will said, "And hide my box braids?" and got out.

He stood on the boardwalk, looking at the beach where some waited at the water's edge for small waves to wet them. As a few more walked by him, he checked the time on his phone. The boardwalk was clear when he began to walk, cognizant of careless security workers. At midnight, Will went onto the beach to search. He walked up and down the water's edge, stopping once to feed the seagulls crumbs from his pockets. On his way back to the boardwalk was when he found Homeless Man Twenty drinking below it.

Will walked up to him asking, "Do you always drink alone?"

"Another teenager, ay?"

"My parents would've killed me if they caught me drinking when they were alive."

Homeless Man Twenty tossed him a beer and said, "Well, cheers to them! No toast, just drink it," and he did.

"Tastes better than liquor. That's for sure," as he looked around.

He said, "Well, I'm sure you know more about baseball with that bat than you do about drugs and alcohol having had good parents, ay?"

"Do you know anything about baseball?"

"I love the game," he threw up, "but I could never hit the ball hard enough to hit a home run."

"The key is not to swing so hard," taking another look around.

"Show me."

Will said, "Sure," and swung at his head before beating him to death.

Part 6: Life

The graduates of Venoa Beach High gathered on the marina, which was crowded with men and women also in their bathing suits, basking in the sun with young bodies to brag about. Jessica wore a wrap skirt to match her mango yellow bikini and welcomed everyone over a cordless microphone before The Riot performed. With her hair wet, Becca sang, moving to the rhythm. The guys whistled at her appeal in lace pants while the females encouraged her with screams. Pretty Patty ignored the passes from older men but found herself dancing between two of them too tipsy to move away. Other females embraced the edgy males stealing dances with them with a touch of their hand. As two were kissing, passing illegal pills to each other with their tongues, another poured half a beer on their body before drinking the rest. The Scooter Crew took turns smashing empty beer cans on their heads. When Superman tossed three full ones to The Skate Lords, the rival crew was reticent to drink them until Scooter approached them with a fist pump to further their plan.

Mike said, "We never said sorry."

"For what, bro?"

"Your loss," he said and drank. "Scott was the chosen one."

"Bro, we consider this a celebration of his life," said Scooter.

"Are you guys getting on the yacht?"

"Of course, bro! Aren't you guys going?"

"Not our style," he said and drank some more.

"Well, we probably won't see you after the cruise, so we should do lunch and talk extreme sports."

"It would be an honor."

Scooter said, "Al's Eatery on the state road," and put a folded paper with the date and time in Mike's pocket.

Part 7: Dates

The crowd cheered for The Riot.

Over the microphone, Becca said, "If you guys don't leave here tonight with a date for next weekend, something's seriously wrong with you."

A male was walking on his hands through the crowd when Neglected Nikki appeared in a high waist cross strap bikini set, beaming with as much pride as Becca had singing.

"You know, red looks good on you," said an older guy, "and it's also my favorite color."

Will said, "It's also the color of blood."

As the older guy back petaled away, she asked, "Are you going to intimidate every guy that tries to talk to me?"

"Where's Fat Matt? I actually like him," he said.

"Why don't you just date me already?"

Will said, "You're too sweet," looking around.

"Who are you looking for?"

"A friend," he said. "You don't know her."

She folded her arms and shouted, "Her?!" before storming off.

Meanwhile, The Makeup Misses were planning to co-host a dating game with Jessica during intermission.

Part 8: Games

Erica handpicked three guys while Liz passed out tickets to females who took Becca's message to heart. The crowd cheered when Jessica announced the raffle winner who raced to the microphone ready to choose her date. She wore a white one-piece with a sun hat and studded shades, blocking the rays streaming through clouds on a day as hot as she was looking. The brunette was introducing herself when Will approached Pretty Patty from behind.

"You were right," he said, surprising her.

"Guys tend to tell me I'm right about everything when I look this hot," she said, as he spun her around for another look. She wore a black ring linked halter bikini with shining skin from her shoulders to the white tips on her toes.

"That's a game they're playing with you."

"And you don't play games?"

"I've been honest so far," said Will. "The games guys play usually involve lies."

"We all lie," said Pretty Patty.

"Well, if you don't see value in my honesty, then you're probably not worth my time."

"Well," she flipped her hair, "if you see less value in my looks than you do in getting to know me, then you're definitely worth mine," as they walked to the nearest cooler. Will opened her beer before guzzling his own. They were laughing at a bearded guy choking on beer flowing from no ordinary bong when Bobby appeared.

He said, "Come here," and Pretty Patty went.

Will blurted, "Wait!"

"She was just toying with you," said Bobby. "She likes attention."

"She likes *my* attention," said Will.

He laughed asking, "You think you're a better man than me?"

"I think she thinks I could be."

Bobby stood face to face with Will and said, "You're looking into the eyes of a killer, boy."

He said, "So are you."

Part 9: Eyes

Half the crowd danced to The Riot while others mingled. Pretty Patty sat on Bobby's shoulders eyeing Will who stood alone drinking. The Scooter Crew scattered after Fat Matt followed Neglected Nikki into the bathroom. When they came out, there were females waiting in line for a touch-up from The Makeup Misses.

Liz said, "We literally should've taken donations," while doing someone's makeup.

Erica said, "Now that this one's done," and closed her makeup kit, "we're only doing *eyes*," as another two females sat.

"That's what's going to get them laid anyway."

"It's all in the eyes," as Jessica came in with a bucket full of bills.

"Are you coming to pee or pay to get your eyes done?"

Jessica said, "They're donations," and grabbed Erica's eyeliner to assist them.

"You literally had to be in our heads," said Erica.

"Makeup minds think alike."

"You've got a nice touch," said Liz, watching Jessica.

"Your makeup mind would make a great Makeup Miss."

"Really?"

Liz said, "She's too good."

Jessica exclaimed, "I literally am planning to have sex with my best friend's ex-boyfriend!"

"Because you're bad?" asked Erica.

"Because I go after what I want."

Rosemary stuck her head in and said, "Everyone's waiting for you three to start boarding!"

Jessica and The Makeup Misses stuffed cash in their bathing suits before running out the bathroom toward the yacht. The large vessel stood out among the small boats docked next to it. Erica was counting everyone in line to board when The Bass Boys appeared at the end.

"Graduates only," said Erica.

Blake made eye contact with Jessica who said, "They can come."

Part 10: Contact

While underway, the pool brought life out the older teenagers as they splashed and swam, racing from one side to the other yelling out obscenities for fun. Fat Matt chose a movie to cuddle with Neglected Nikki after she and Will followed The Scooter Crew onboard going unnoticed. They sat among others in the cinema snacking while most of the boys played basketball on a separate deck. As The Makeup Misses were tanning with Rosemary in the beach club where The Bass Boys were lounging waterside, Jessica was lazing on the private deck with Becca and Harry.

"I'm pregnant again," and covered her face.

Jessica asked, "Really?!"

"And we're dating," said Harry.

"You have to tell Blake," she said as she slid into her flip flops.

"For what? We haven't been in contact, so he's moved on!"

"For closure!"

Becca stood up asking, "You mean he's here?!"

"Yes," going to find him.

While arguing about what to say, Becca and Harry followed her. Jessica blocked the television to ask The Scooter Crew where he was. When they shrugged, she checked by the pool. With

Becca behind her sweating, she ran into The Makeup Misses in robes.

"Have you seen Blake?"

"Who's Blake?" asked Liz.

"Tall, *cute* white boy," said Jessica. "He hangs out with another really tall Black guy and two other boys one inch above six feet."

Erica said, "Oh, they're waterside," and Jessica rushed there with Becca's wrist in hand.

Harry was standing behind his new girlfriend when Blake said, "I was just about to come find you to talk."

"He wants to know why," said Fish.

"Tell him," said Jessica.

"I was pregnant with Harry's baby while we were together and got rid of it. Now that him and I are together, I'm pregnant again."

Haywood asked, "Wait, what?!"

"It's Jess's fault!" Becca exclaimed. "She set me up with Harry because she liked you! She knew he and I would like each other because we both do music!"

Jessica slapped Becca.

Blake said, "Now, we're both hurting."

Harry said, "I'll heal her tonight. What's pain without pleasure, right?"

"Watch your mouth, man."

Harry was standing toe to toe with Big Ant when he said, "You're not that tough."

Haywood stepped between them saying, "I play a contact sport, so try me."

The boldest Bass Boy ducked Harry's blow before suplexing him into the water. The drummer swam back to the moving boat while Haywood splashed around.

Fish exclaimed, "He can't swim!" and jumped in.

Jessica ran to the cockpit screaming, "Stop the boat!"

"You're going to be champion!" swimming for Haywood's life.

"Hold on, man!"

Blake said, *"Why aren't we stopping?"* as Haywood drowned.

Story 13
Neighbors Of
Venoa Farms

Part 1: Back

"Bobby, clean this mess for your father, will you, dear?" Helen said while exercising in the living room.

"He throws a welcome back party for me and wants me to clean up after *his* friends?" as he searched for a trash bag.

"Mayor Mark is your friend, too," breathing heavy. "He ate school lunch with you freshman year, remember?"

"Yea," said Bobby, "at least he has seen me wrestle," slamming the bottom cabinet.

The star athlete stared at a picture of he and The Barrel before throwing it in the trash bag. After tossing cups and dumping ash trays with half smoked cigars, he sat on the sofa motivating his mother throughout her sets. He showed her how to do a push up before pulling out the vacuum. When he finished cleaning, he went upstairs to his room where Pretty Patty was unpacking his suitcase.

"Your mom let me in an hour ago."

Bobby said, "Did you like that kid?" with piercing eyes.

"How am I going to like somebody I just met?"

He grabbed her by the throat and said, "Don't toy with me. If you want out, say it."

"Let go of me," and he did.

"You didn't want me to come back," said Bobby, "so you can talk to a lot of guys to know what a whore feels like."

She slapped him and stormed out.

Part 2: Feelings

The Meddling Man parked his golf cart in the street.

"You can't leave that there, sir!" exclaimed Pretty Patty out her car window as she was backing out.

"I saw you swinging your arms as you walked out," he said, chewing on hay. "Would you mind telling me what a pretty girl like you is doing so upset?"

"My boyfriend who's back from college in Major City."

"So, a quarrel is my intuitive guess on why."

Bobby yelled out his bedroom window, "Bitch!"

"Asshole!"

The Meddling Man exclaimed, "Now, I'm going to have to ask you, son of The Barrel to come out here, so I can hear both sides!"

Bobby shut his window.

"He's careless with my feelings," she said.

"Now," said The Meddling Man, "calling you out your name and slamming windows are what we call red flags."

"He has a good side."

"So, does my wild boar Billy," he said, and spat, "but do you see me cutting him loose?"

"No, sir."

"Now, if I see you over here again, I'll be sure to have Billy tied to my cart in case he puts his hands on you."

She lied, "He won't," turning the ignition.

The Meddling Man rode away thinking, "I've got a bad feeling about that young man."

Meanwhile, Bobby was on the phone.

"Real men cheat," he said.

Part 3: Real

Will recorded Uncle Moe dancing while hanging paintings in his new home. As the dropout tried holding his phone steady, dodging the boxes stacked on the floor, Neglected Nikki read Davey a book. Will took over babysitting him after Graves was killed, collecting memories instead of money. When Neglected Nikki's phone rang, he stopped recording to listen. Fat Matt told her how important she was to furthering their plan. When she ignored Will after he asked her about it, he became aroused by her strength. She hung up eager to finish the story as Davey was dancing with Uncle Moe to kill time.

Will was upstairs in his room when he thought, "Nikki may be sweet, but she's real," looking out the window.

Neglected Nikki came in.

"I'm going to miss you," she said and laid on his bed.

He licked his lips and said, "How badly?"

"Badly enough to tell you."

"Badly enough to show me?" and he laid on top of her.

She rolled her eyes saying, "I'm taken," and stood to stretch.

"Fat Matt?"

"You said you liked him."

Will opened the window and screamed in frustration, startling neighbors outside walking for afternoon exercise. Neglected Nikki was leaving when Pretty Patty stepped out her car parked at the house across the street. Will did a double take before checking himself in the mirror.

Part 4: Check

While firing at the bullseye in the backyard with a pistol, Bobby listened to his father brag about owning the only business in Venoa Beach with a sister store in Major City. The Barrel laughed, checking the length of the barrel of his newest shotgun for bulges. When he was finished inspecting it, he inserted rounds. Bobby watched to learn before stepping aside to see him shoot it.

After the first round, Bobby said, "Howey's missing."

"Yea, and?" still firing.

"Danny committed suicide."

The Barrel stopped aiming to say, "Don't you go getting weak on me, Bobby. Did you cry?"

"No," he said, "but I checked on their families."

"Good man," said The Barrel. "Not a real man, but a good one."

"What's the difference?"

"A real man's emotions are buried too deep even for condolences, and a good man shows his emotions assuming people will benefit from his truth."

"What's wrong with that?"

"Well," said The Barrel, reloading, "people are liars, making them more willing to take advantage your emotions than to empathize with you, understand?"

Bobby said, "Nobody has ever taken advantage of me."

"Because you haven't met the woman who you *think* is the woman of your dreams who will."

"Patty's good to me."

"She's good to you to blind you."

Bobby tucked his pistol in his pants saying, "I'm going to check on her."

Part 5: Blind

Will was looking at his reflection in Pretty Patty's car window when The Meddling Man rode by. When the dropout waved, his new neighbor pumped the breaks and backed in the driveway.

He took the strand of hay out his mouth and spat before asking, "What do you teens call that hair style?"

"Box braids," said Will.

"With fun hair like that, you're just what she needs."

"Who's she?"

"The girl whose house you're at."

"Her name's Patty. She didn't tell me that. I read her name tag at the sporting goods store by the beach."

"So, you're here to see if she remembers you. That's my intuitive guess."

"She has a boyfriend."

The Meddling Man said, "Now, don't let that stop you because their love ain't blind like my eyes on a book without reading glasses."

Pretty Patty opened the front door.

"Hey," said Will.

"Now, I'm going to leave you two alone, but I want to hear all about your reunification when I see one of you again."

She said, "Reunification?"

The Meddling Man said, "I know where you live," and rode away.

"Nice golf cart," said Will.

"How did you find me?"

"I live across the street," he said.

*

They stood outside play fighting before Bobby pulled up in his custom pickup with heavy metal music so loud Uncle Moe stuck his head out to see. With shades over his eyes, he slammed the door behind him and pulled out his pistol. Pretty Patty panicked while Will stood still staring into his eyes.

Aiming at point blank range, Bobby said, "So, you're a true Venoan."

"My death is always a consequence," he said.

"So, is the death of someone else," and he aimed at Pretty Patty.

Will tackled him.

Pretty Patty screamed, "Stop, please!" as the boys fought for the gun.

"I'm going to kill you, boy!"

Uncle Moe came outside.

"You guys break it up," he said, rushing over unaware of the weapon.

The gun fired.

Will screamed, "No!" as his uncle collapsed and died.

Part 6: Yes

Pretty Patty's parents wrapped their arms around her as medics put Uncle Moe's body onto the ambulance. Will sat on the curb with

Neglected Nikki who was steady wiping his tears. Helen was standing beside Bobby when Chief Earl approached them after shaking hands with The Barrel.

"Your father says that you're on scholarship, son?"

"Yes, sir."

Chief Earl said, "Then, the gun wasn't yours."

"It was *his*," he said, pointing at Will.

The Barrel said, "He knows that, don't you, Earl?"

With Bobby's father behind him, Chief Earl approached The Dropouts to read Will his rights.

"How old are you, son?"

"Seventeen," he said.

"Son, you have a right to remain silent."

"What?"

"Federal law prohibits anyone under eighteen from possessing a handgun."

Neglected Nikki yelled, "It wasn't his!" as Will was handcuffed.

"Yes, it was," said The Barrel, smiling.

"No, it wasn't!"

"Yes, it was!"

Pretty Patty rushed over saying, "No, it wasn't!"

Bobby grabbed her and asked, "Whose side are you on?!"

"You were going to kill me!"

Will was sitting in the backseat of Chief Earl's SUV when The Meddling Man appeared with Billy. He parked his golf cart and untied his wild boar who sniffed its surroundings. Bobby backed up as Billy came close.

"Get that thing away from me!"

"I'll make a deal with you," said The Meddling Man. "If you stay away from her, he'll stay away from you."

Chief Earl asked, "What's the meaning of this?"

"Now, officer, there's a few things I need to know before I can tie Billy up."

"This is none of your business," said The Barrel.

"As neighbor of that fine young man in custody, I would say that yes, it is my concern. Now, I want to know what's going on."

"He was carrying a gun that accidentally killed a man."

The Meddling Man said, "I don't believe you."

"You don't have to," said The Barrel.

He stood face to face with him and said, "If you want business in this town, you will tell the truth."

"If you want to live, you will go home."

The Meddling Man smiled.

Part 7: Truth

Helen was cooking dinner when The Barrel's phone rang.

"Hello, stunning," he said over the phone.

As he started to whisper, she stopped stirring to listen. When he laughed louder than the sizzle, she banged the cookware on the pot and scowled at her husband.

He looked and said, "I'll call you, later."

"Was that her?"

"We've been together too long for you be jealous," as he prepared his own plate.

"You make me feel so unattractive!"

"That's not my intent, Helen."

"You're not a real man," she said, "because a real man would tell me the truth. You're not attracted to me anymore!"

"Well, you can't leave," said The Barrel, "because it'll make me look bad."

Meanwhile, Bobby was standing outside Pretty Patty's house with a box of chocolates. After ringing the doorbell several times, she came to the door barefoot with her sleeves rolled up. She ate the chocolates where she stood and picked her teeth with her nails.

"What's gotten into you?"

She said, "Living my truth," wiping chocolate off her cheek with her shirt.

Bobby's phone rang.

He said, "Hello, stunning," over the phone.

Pretty Patty snatched it from him and asked, "Who are you?"

A female spoke.

Bobby said, "She appreciates a real man."

"I never wanted a real man. I wanted the real you," and slammed the front door in his face.

Part 8: Men

The Barrel passed Chief Earl a beer.

"I'm going to put a big screen TV right out here on the patio," said Bobby's father, taking sips.

After taking the Chief of Police on a tour of his house, The Barrel lit a cigar on the sofa with his feet up. Chief Earl sat in a recliner with his second beer while Mayor Mark stood flipping through channels. They agreed to watch sports news before Helen walked in with cookies. She looked Chief Earl in the eyes and offered Mayor Mark more than one. The Barrel was unaware.

"How's the married life treating you?" asked Chief Earl, eyeing Helen in the kitchen.

The Barrel said, "She cooks, she cleans, and isn't mean," and laughed.

"So, it's perfect, huh?"

"My aim is the only thing perfect," said Mayor Mark, making eye contact with Helen.

"We've been together for twenty-two years."

Chief Earl said, "That's long enough to have had more than one child."

Helen brought him another beer.

Mayor Mark said, "Children are expensive."

"So were my new *guns*," said The Barrel, getting up. "Let's go out back for a few rounds."

Helen thought, "That's men for ya."

The three of them passed guns back and forth shooting in the sky before aiming at the bullseye. With a cigar hanging out his mouth, The Barrel would reload. Mayor Mark spun his pistol in hand after every shot while Chief Earl rewarded himself with a sip every time he hit the center. The Barrel was showing off his newest shotgun when Chief Earl went inside claiming to have to use the bathroom.

Meanwhile, Helen was washing dishes.

"Hello," said Chief Earl.

She said, "Intuitive."

He went in his wallet saying, "Then, here's my card," and walked out after handing it to her.

The Barrel was aiming two pistols at the bullseye when Bobby appeared.

"Can I have a shot?"

"Nope," said The Barrel. "Today, it's real men only."

Part 9: Shot

The Meddling Man drove around Venoa Farms to keep an eye on Pretty Patty as she was running for exercise. The lawns were mowed and wet from the sprinklers that sprayed her as she went by. Some houses were lit as if neighbors were awake for an evening snack. The Meddling Man would stop to see. Pretty Patty was catching her breath outside one of those homes when Bobby appeared in sweats.

"Breathe through your nose," he said.

"What are you doing out here?"

"Working out," he said, smiling.

"No, what are you really doing out here?"

Bobby said, "I want another shot," as they started to jog.

"Then, turn yourself in."

"I'm scared to lose my scholarship."

Pretty Patty said, "Venoans don't fear consequences."

They were turning the corner when they ran into The Meddling Man who pumped his breaks. He got out, tossed his straw hat on the seat, and spat with a strand of hay hanging out his mouth. Bobby extended his hand.

"Now, do you know what my handshake means, son?"

Bobby put his hand down and said, "No, sir."

He said, "My handshake *means*," looking into his eyes, "that I see and respect your truth enough to work with you, having proved your influence over the good as now a man of substance."

"I work with my dad."

"I'm not offering you a job, son. I'm offering you one shot to tell those officers the truth like a good man would," said The Meddling Man, "because a good man… is a real man."

"What about my scholarship?"

"Have your coach call me," he said and extended his hand.

Part 10: Bad

Helen brought Bobby his food humming while The Barrel prepared his own plate. When the small business owner sat at the kitchen table, he removed Bobby's headphones off his head.

"Listen," and Bobby did.

As she sat with them humming after every bite, The Barrel was texting his mistress, showing off her messages to his son. Helen's eyes were on her plate until Bobby knocked his father's phone out his hand.

"Bobby!" she exclaimed.

The Barrel slapped him.

Bobby hit him back and said, "I'm better than you."

They were both standing when The Barrel said, "Show me."

Bobby followed his father to the backyard with Helen behind him with his shirt in her hands.

As they stood on the grass, Bobby asked, "Are you sure about this, old man?"

"I want to see who you are," swinging his fist. Bobby felt the blow and landed his own punch. The Barrel went for his legs to ground him. When he realized Bobby was too strong, he backed away prepared to throw punches instead. Bobby dodged the blow to go around him for a rear body lock take down.

"You're a bad man," and let him up.

While catching his breath, he asked, "Do you want to know why I've never seen you wrestle?"

"Why?"

"Because I had a son for myself, not for himself, understand?" and loaded his shotgun.

"What are you doing?"

The Barrel said, "Realizing that I don't need you anymore," and aimed at him.

He pulled the trigger when Helen screamed, "No!"

Bobby collapsed and died.

Story 14
What Happens Off
State Road 1

Part 1: Hero

Fish was crying out loud, Big Ant was kicking up cemetery dirt, and Blake was trying to calm them. With their eyes red, they huddled up, encouraging each other to be strong. Engraved on Haywood's tombstone was his nickname Hero. On the ground below it were flowers from Lady of Red and others like Asian Brenda. Jessica left her cheerleading uniform, promising to root for underdogs like he was before learning to wrestle. When Fish said he was going to join the wrestling team, The Bass Boys did their handshake in Haywood's memory. Fish put on the boldest Bass Boy's ear guards that were lying there and spat.

*

The Bass Boys were slap boxing among themselves when Will appeared from afar holding Pretty Patty's hand.

Fish said, "Wait, that isn't Bobby."

"He was at the extreme, man."

"And on the yacht," as the couple was walking toward them.

"Let's see what he says," said Blake.

Will introduced Pretty Patty.

"We know who she is," said Fish.

She said, "We just wanted to share our condolences."

"Who is he?" asked Blake.

"My hero."

"Just call me Will," he said with red eyes.

Part 2: Eyes

Will walked in Venoa Beach Gun & Pawn wiping gloss off his lips.

"Welcome," said The Barrel.

"I just came by to say thank you."

"A real man doesn't say thank you because he knows most people do good things for others for themselves."

"Why does it matter why people do good things for others?"

"Motive," he said.

"Well, everyone can't be real with everybody."

Helen appeared and said, "It's all in the eyes if you want to know if they are because even someone's actions can deceive you."

Will left thinking, "Trust nobody."

Mayor Mark walked in with a shotgun over his right shoulder and Woman Supreme on his left side. Helen hugged the mayor's secretary as the men shook hands.

Mayor Mark asked, "Have they found Bobby?" following The Barrel into his office.

"The last time I saw him he had the eyes of cold-blooded killer."

"Do you think he would've shot that young man Earl let go?"

"I let him go," said The Barrel and sat, "because I told the truth."

Mayor Mark stood with his back turned saying, "That's why we want to give you a key to the city. Here, at your store."

"I should already have one as long as we we've been friends."

"Friends share their truth."

The Barrel said, "The truth is I'm a real man. Who else would you call on to support a strong, Black man like you in your effort to run Venoa Beach?"

Mayor Mark laughed.

Part 3: Strong

There was a line inside Al's Eatery when Will walked in with Pretty Patty, who rushed over to Neglected Nikki as she untied her apron for her lunch break.

"We're wearing the exact same sneakers!" exclaimed Pretty Patty, sliding in the booth with her.

Will came over and said, "I need your keys."

"Where are Mrs. Greta and Mr. Gary?!"

"Date night," they said.

"Again?"

"Real love never gets old," said Will.

"And a strong bond never breaks," said Neglected Nikki, tossing him the keys.

Meanwhile, The Scooter Crew walked in.

"He's on his way, bro," ending the call.

"Sweet."

"This is too easy, brother," said Superman.

Fat Matt asked, "Do you see Nikki?"

"Over there," said Scooter, pointing.

The Scooter Crew skipped line when Neglected Nikki noticed them and followed her to a table they reserved away from the crowd. Will saluted Fat Matt before hugging his friend goodbye. As he and Pretty Patty were leaving, Mike walked in popping ketamine pills.

He thought, "What would I do without these?" as he walked to the table.

"Mike, how are you, bro?"

"Just trying to live with myself."

"Stay strong," said Fat Matt, signaling to Neglected Nikki.

"Nice tattoo, brother!"

"My sister Rosemary did it."

"We see her at the mall all the time," said Scooter.

"She's sweet."

Neglected Nikki said, "Decided, boys?" smiling.

Part 4: Decisions

After ordering his food, Mike went to the bathroom where Angel was using a urinal.

"When you have to go, you have to go," said the skater, standing at the one beside him.

"Your body decides, si? Though most decisions are our own, and if the bad ones we make don't excite us as much as they frustrate us, then we're doomed for regret, which weighs a ton."

"What's there to be excited about?"

Angel said, "*Insight*," and flushed the urinal.

"I'm not that deep."

"If you were," he said, washing his hands, "then you would realize that you're always being taught."

"Why is that?" asked Mike, flushing.

"So, that you will make better decisions. Ones based on who you are, si?"

Mike said, "I killed a guy," unable to look himself in the mirror.

"Without strength, you have also killed yourself," said Angel, drying his hands.

"I'm still alive," said Mike, washing his hands.

"Some deaths start within."

Meanwhile, Neglected Nikki was in the kitchen putting rat poison in Mike's food. She brought the boys their orders as the skater was walking back to his chair. He sat down and stuffed his face with the rest of them until he fell on the floor and died.

"Call 911!" yelled The Scooter Crew.

Part 5: Fall

As the ambulance drove past with Scooter's cargo van behind it, Pretty Patty sat on the picnic table outside The Service Station waiting for Will who was inside. She wiped the gloss off her lips to put another flavor on. After letting her hair down, guys at the gas pumps whistled and waved at her. She rolled her eyes before blowing them a kiss. When Will walked out with two slurpees and beef jerky hanging out his mouth, Pretty Patty adjusted her shorts and flipped her hair. He asked her to go in his pocket to check the receipt and count change. After she did, he told her to put it in her purse. While sitting down, they drank their slurpees after Will made a toast to Graves.

"If he was so smart, why did he dropout?"

"He was a reader," he said.

"Shouldn't that make him want to stay?"

"Well, once you learn how to read, you can learn whatever you want."

"He just wasn't interested in the subjects."

Will said, "We both would fall asleep."

"I could fall asleep right now," she said, "not because I'm bored, but because I'm comfortable."

Will asked, "Are you falling for me?" squinting at her.

"I've already fell," she said, putting her head on his shoulder.

When Fish drove up with the music blasting, Pretty Patty picked her head up as the bass was booming above treble like it always was. Fish was parked at the gas pump when Blake got out the car and walked toward the station entrance. He spat like Haywood and gave Will a head nod before going inside.

Blake thought. "He can break our fall."

Part 6: Broken

Big Ant was pumping gas when Blake walked out.

"Tell Fish to turn it down!"

Will said, "You guys should keep it turned up."

Blake asked, "Why?" coming closer to the couple.

"For the vibes," said Will.

"But then, I couldn't hear what you had to say."

"About what?"

"Take a ride with us."

"Why me?"

"We met at a cemetery, so you must have been broken like we were."

Pretty Patty encouraged Will to go as Fish drove up to the picnic table with Big Ant in the front seat, bobbing to the bass that boomed in his head. When Blake got in, so did Will after whispering something in his girlfriend's ear. The dropout rode with The Bass Boys down State Road 1 to Lily's Greenhouse where Sierra was working.

Part 7: Green

Lily welcomed the boys inside where they breathed in oxygen from her plants.

"Oceans may be blue, love," she said, "but land is *green*."

Blake said. "Green is the color of rebirth."

"Renewal, man," as they pet the ones they were unfamiliar with. Fish was smelling the hyacinth in his hands when Sierra offered to assist him.

"Check these out," showing him the bright zinnias.

"Venoa Oaks, right?"

"Sierra," she said, extending her hand.

"Got any money leftover?" as they shook hands.

"After bombarding the arcade, my boys and I spent it on Video Game Design Camp."

"Your boys?"

"Haven't you heard of Sierra and The C Students? We're next to run this town after you tall boys of course."

"If I was a C student," said Will, "I would be playing college baseball next year."

Sierra said, "You're the first baseball player I've seen in here."

"We're here for his girl," said Blake.

"Then, I've got the perfect flower."

Will followed Sierra past the common flowers to the exotic ones she said would get his girlfriend to grovel at his feet. He complimented her colorful knee-high socks and sneakers, convincing her there was a boy out there who matches her style.

"I'm serious," said Will.

"As serious as you are about your girlfriend?"

"She's my air."

"Then, check out these orchids."

Will pointed and said, "What about this?"

"That's the blue passionflower."

Part 8: Passion

Fish dropped Will off at Venoa Beach Hotel where Pretty Patty sat waiting for him in the lobby. With his arms full of flowers, he walked through the sliding doors focused on her. She rushed over to smell them and took one to put in her hair. On the elevator, she blushed as he was licking his lips. He walked backwards onto the seventh floor, keeping his eyes on her as she walked like a model down the hall. When he opened their room door, she scurried inside, tossing the flowers on the bed. They ran into each other's arms and started kissing, as the petals' scent carried throughout the room.

Will pulled away and asked, "Ever had a first time like this?"

"Bobby was my first, so what do you think?"

"They still haven't found him," he said, kissing her neck.

"What if he's dead?"

Will asked, "Who would kill him?" taking off his shirt.

"I don't know."

"What else didn't you like about him besides the obvious?"

They fell on the bed naked before she said, "No passion."

As they rolled around on top of the sheets kissing, police lights were flashing through the windows. Mayor Mark and the workers at City Hall were being escorted in their cars down State Road 1. When the teenagers heard the sirens, they stood up to look. As Mayor Mark waved, they cheered before jumping back into bed.

"I wonder what's going on," said Will, while they were having sex.

Pretty Patty said, "Let's find out," catching her breath.

Part 9: Newfound

Venoa Beach Gun & Pawn was surrounded by police cars and people on foot who parked nearby to see The Barrel receive a key to the city. Sitting beside Chief Earl behind the podium was Helen. Next to her was Woman Supreme, who offered The Barrel some wine from her purse as Mayor Mark was helping him adjust his tie.

When he refused a drink and slid her his phone number instead, she whispered to his wife, "Real men have business cards," and crumbled the piece of paper.

Meanwhile, Lady of Red was passing out her own business cards as the newest florist in Major City.

"You're moving?" a woman asked her.

"Yes."

"When do you open?"

"Soon," said Lady of Red, "but you can go ahead place your order online."

The Bass Boys appeared with Messy Molly and Latina Selena.

"So, this is where you stand if you're gorgeous," Fish said, hugging his neighbor.

"You look amazing."

"Muy bien."

Blake said, "Hey, we want you to meet somebody!"

"He's just like Haywood, man."

"Haywood 2.0!"

Lady of Red said, "Well, where is your newfound friend?"

Will surprised Big Ant from behind.

Blake said, "This is him!"

"Nice hair."

"Nice face," he said.

Pretty Patty and the girls whispered among themselves as Woman Supreme settled the crowd. When Mayor Mark took to the podium, there was complete silence.

"As Venoans, we are not defined by our wrong doings, but by our reason behind them."

Someone shouted, "We love you, Mayor Mark!"

Over the microphone, he told The Barrel, "Tell the people your reason behind killing your son?"

The Barrel looked over at Helen as he was being handcuffed.

"After all these years!"

"Then, Helen, you tell the people what you're going to do with your newfound freedoms?"

She grabbed the microphone and said, "This shop is closed."

Part 10: Open

Fish stopped at a red light on State Road 1.

As Messy Molly played in his hair, he thought, "Me, my girl, and the open road."

With no other cars in sight, he rolled the windows down for his girlfriend to scream as she always did. As the light turned green, he hit the gas, screeching his tires for a few feet until switching lanes. Messy Molly encouraged his speed, shouting at the brisk wind of nature to get out the way. While there was no traffic, he ran red lights and made U-turns in the street speeding in both directions.

"Wait, there's a cop!"

"Where?!" he said, looking behind him.

A semi-truck appeared in front of them.

"Turn around!" she screamed before they crashed.

Messy Molly died with her mouth open.

Story 15
What Happens
Senior Year

Part 1: Champions

A new pit of vipers was painted on the far wall of the gymnasium where Blake and Big Ant stood breathing heavy near the baseline among the other members of the varsity basketball team. When Coach RJ blew his whistle, they ran the length of the court for the last time. He passed the ball to Blake to captain one group of five and chose Big Ant to lead another set. With their teams in separate color practice uniforms, they led them to center court where Coach RJ stood.

"We made it, gentlemen," he said.

Blake said, "Just one more game, guys."

"And we're champions," said someone else.

"No, we're already champions," said Coach RJ, "and all we have to do is show it one more time."

"Hands in, man."

The coach said, "Champions on three."

Blake counted.

"Champions!" they shouted.

As they scrimmaged, Coach RJ called out offensive sets while Assistant Coach Aaron encouraged defense. Blake whispered Haywood's name after every shot. When he scored, he would spit on his hand and rub the bottom of his sneakers for traction. Big Ant caught the ball off the rim with one hand, dunking over his teammates after growing three more inches. The six foot nine Bass Boy demanded the ball, touching it for an easy basket every time down the floor. The score was tied when Blake banked the game-winning floater coming off a solid screen.

"Good run, gentlemen!"

Blake and Big Ant were doing their handshake on the sidelines when Asian Brenda came in pushing Fish in a wheelchair.

Part 2: Push

Fish's phone rang.

He said, "It's Jessica," and passed it to Blake.

"Hello?"

"Ask her if she's coming to the game, man."

Blake said, "Of course she's coming to see her boyfriend light it up from three-point range."

Jessica cheered over the phone.

Blake was ending his conversation when Big Ant said, "Tell her to bring an entourage, man."

"So, what did she want?" asked Fish.

"To tell me how much fun she's having with Pretty Patty now that they've reconciled," said Blake.

"Yay!" exclaimed Asian Brenda. "Friends forever!"

While the rest of the team was heading to the locker room, Blake and Big Ant followed Asian Brenda and Fish into the gymnasium lobby where the trophy case was. The boys stared at Haywood's wrestling photos while Asian Brenda wiped her tears. Fish was pushed to his breaking point after reaching Will's voicemail.

"The Bass Boys are dead!" he exclaimed, throwing his phone.

Blake said, "He's probably got a renter. Business is booming."

"Yea, man, chill out."

"Chill out?! Our best friend is dead because of me, my girlfriend is dead because of me, and I'm paralyzed because of *me*!"

"Haywood's dead because of me!" Blake shouted.

"I could've saved him!"

"It was destiny, man."

"I could've changed his destiny!"

Blake said, "We never should've been on the boat anyway."

"Yea," said Fish, "you and your whore of an ex-girlfriend."

"That's true, man."

Blake said, "No, I agree."

After overhearing their argument, Coach RJ approached them saying, "Some of the best insight you will ever receive will come from dealing with the opposite sex."

"What have you learned, coach?" asked Blake.

"Push each other to be better, because nothing makes less sense than being in relationship where both of you refuse to grow."

Part 3: Better

After Asian Brenda left, Fish waited in the gymnasium for his friends to finish changing in the locker room. The cheerleaders were practicing their routines at center court while he held a medicine ball over his head, pretending to be as strong as Haywood was. Among the girls was Latina Selena who was proud to show off her promise ring to her squad. Big Ant warned her that his feelings could change as a top recruit, attracting girls from college campuses near and far. The yo-yoing Bass Boy owned a large luxury SUV after Coach RJ negotiated with recruiters. With their money from renting out the trawler, Blake, Big Ant, and Will put a wheelchair lift in it with a side-entry ramp for Fish.

"Who better than The Bass Boys to run this city?" asked Blake, boastful after a hot shower.

"Major City is next, man," drying his face.

Fish said, "Admit it, guys. Things haven't been the same without Haywood and it never will be!"

"After Haywood died, and then Molly in the crash, man, things can only get better."

"We're better because of our loses. Will's waiting for us on the pier."

"He's not one of us! Does he even know the handshake?"

"It was *his* idea to put the lift in the SUV!"

"Oh, well, let's just eat. Maybe I'll feel better after a drink from Julianne."

Part 4: Jewels

Rick's Restaurant was full of empty chairs and spotless tabletops maintained by bussers who Julianne would signal to wipe the bar between breaks. When Will and The Bass Boys came in, she removed a chair from the closest table to the bar for Fish to park his wheelchair. After the boys ordered their food, she brought them each a beer, announcing to everyone that their twenty-first birthdays had passed to cover herself. Fish guzzled his.

Blake said, "He needs another one."

"Still mourning?" asked Julianne.

"I don't think I'll ever stop."

She said, "Well, I don't think death is as bad as people think it is."

Will asked, "Why do you think people think that?"

"Because they're not *true* Venoans," as she rushed back behind the bar to tend to a guest shaking his cup.

Will showed them the receipts for the day while Big Ant signed autographs, pretending to be a professional athlete home after a road game. He took pictures with them, showing off his jewels before Fish demanded his attention. They were laughing at him when Blake went outside for air followed by Julianne.

"Need a woman's perspective?" she asked.

"Senior year's supposed to be fun."

"And instead, it's painful."

"Haywood didn't deserve to die."

Julianne said, "No true Venoan ever does."

After responding to a text message from Jessica, he said, "My girlfriend's throwing another party."

"And how do you feel about that?"

"Well, I met Becca at one of them. Haywood died at the last one. So, I was hoping she would do something more intimate with having a boyfriend."

"Did you ask her if she would?"

"Nah," said Blake, "parties are kind of her thing, you know?"

"Always remember, it is better to be respected than to be loved without respect."

"Thanks, Julianne. Still coming to the game?"

She said, "Wouldn't miss it, and call me Jewels."

Part 5: Respect

Principal Jon called The Bass Boys to his office.

While walking there, Big Ant thought, "What does he want, man?"

"He called you, too?" Fish asked.

"He wants all three of us."

Blake parked Fish beside Big Ant who stretched his legs so far in his chair his feet about touched the desk. When Principal Jon walked in laughing, they kept a straight face, causing him to become serious also. With Haywood's file in his hand, he took a deep breath.

"He wasn't that good of a student, but he was becoming one hell of a wrestler."

Fish asked, "Now, you respect him after he's gone? Did you even know him?"

"No," he leaned back in his chair, "but Coach Brock told me you boys were at all his matches."

Blake said, "We skipped practice for some of them."

"What's your point, man?"

"Well, you mentioned respect," he put his feet on the desk, "and for sticking together, you three have mine. Do you know how many friends I had that I wish were still on my journey?"

"Blame yourself," said Fish.

"I do," said Principal Jon, standing up, "and the reason why I'm giving you three the rest of the day off is because I admire the bond you share."

"I'm driving," said Blake.

With his hands in his pockets, he said, "Now, you two ball players have to promise me a championship."

"Promise," they both said, slapping fives.

"And don't tell anybody."

"Man, you're talking to The Bass Boys. We can keep a secret from God."

Part 6: Secret

Officer Todd was annoyed with teenagers harassing workers at kiosks who tried keeping their space neat for those with actual money. When one teenager grabbed their attention, another would grab something off display. He was arresting one when Will and The Bass Boys entered The Food Court.

"I can't believe he gave you guys the day off," said Will, sitting with his chair backwards.

Fish said, "I can't believe that security guard still works here when he should be moved on to bigger and better things."

"You could say the same thing about Jewels," said Blake, pulling out a deck of playing cards.

"Who's Jewels, man?"

"Julianne," he said, shuffling.

Will laughed and said, "You're thinking about her."

"Yea, so what?"

"How would Jessica feel about that?"

While dealing, Blake said, "It's not like that."

"To you it isn't," said Will, counting his cards, "but what about her?"

After playing a few games, Will, Blake, and Fish texted Big Ant their food order while he stood in line. People stopped to meet the six feet nine Bass Boy assuming he was famous. Big Ant played along again, pretending to be a professional athlete. Officer Todd approached him, recognizing who he was and offered to carry his order to his table.

"Big game coming up," he said, as they walked.

"Yea, man."

"When I saw you in the paper and read the box scores, I thought there's no way we could lose!"

Meanwhile, the other three boys sat with their mouths watering.

Will said, "I think Jewels secretly likes you."

"Why do you say that?"

"Because we all have secrets."

Officer Todd sat their food on the table saying, "Enjoy!"

Fish asked, "Officer, what's your secret?"

"You would be surprised how many young women look for older men."

"So, what is it?"

He whispered, "*Cindy*," and walked away.

Part 7: Surprise

"He slept with Cindy?" asked Fish.

Blake said, "I'm not surprised," chewing his food.

"Who's Cindy?" asked Will.

"One of the prettiest girls in school," said Fish, dipping his fries.

"Man, with makeup on she was."

As they ate and talked about girls, young women around Jewels' age eyed their table as they walked past. Some were too shy to wave while others spoke up for their attention. One gave Fish a kiss on the cheek after he complimented her look in high heels. Will was dumping his tray when one approached him.

"Can I braid your hair?"

Will was distracted by an older man standing afar when he thought, "Well, isn't this a surprise."

He pushed chairs out his way trying to get to the older man while Blake called out his name. Will ignored him and hopped over a table eager for a closer look.

He tapped the older man on the shoulder asking, "Where's our machine?"

"What machine?" he asked, turning around.

"Oh, my fault," said Will. "I thought you were someone else."

Part 8: Machine

Will sat back down at the table with his head low.

"Man, who was that guy?"

"I thought he was The Mowing Man."

"Who?" asked Blake with a mouthful.

"The homeless guy from my neighborhood."

Fish asked, "Where did you say you lived again?"

"Venoa Gardens."

Fish exclaimed, "Then, you know the story about The Homicidal Homeowner!"

Will said, "He never existed, but The Mowing Man does."

"What do you want from him?"

"The Crazy Cupid Machine," he said, as Rosemary skated past. She wore a tank top and shorts with a button-down shirt wrapped around her waist. As she showed off her tattoos to bystanders who were captivated by them, Will became inspired.

He approached her asking, "You love art, huh?"

"Yea," she said.

"So, did my Uncle Moe. Is it easy to learn how to tattoo?"

"It's basically tracing, that's all."

"Can you teach me?"

Rosemary said, "If you buy your own machine."

With plans to move her shop into a larger mall in Major City, Rosemary encouraged him to show up often for a lesson.

Part 9: Lesson

As one half ended, the Vipers headed to the locker room. They were down by ten points after struggling to make shots. The other team succeeded at denying Big Ant the ball and capitalized on careless turnovers. Blake and Big Ant shared half the team's points while the others contributed from the foul line. Coach RJ stood calm before his boys as Assistant Coach Aaron reassigned the starting five's defensive assignments to force their opponent to change something that was working for them.

After they sipped water and poured some on their heads to cool off, Coach RJ cleared his throat before saying, "I'm not going to talk about the game."

Someone said, "Why not, coach?"

"Because every game we've played has been a lesson."

"We've learned our lessons," said Blake.

"And now this is the test," said Coach RJ. "Do your teachers give you answers on test day?"

They exclaimed, "No, sir!"

"Then, let's go out there and play like we know the game of basketball."

They ran out the locker room slapping fives before warming up for the second half. Jewels sat on the bottom row of the bleachers as focused as Blake was while Jessica waved at him from the top. Before the buzzer sounded, he ran up to Jewels for advice.

Meanwhile, Jessica was watching.

Part 10: Buzzer

With one minute left and the game tied, Blake walked the ball up the court and called out a set play for Big Ant. He dribbled through the defense and passed it to his friend at the high post. The crowd was standing when he made his move to the basket. When he was fouled, Blake sighed in relief.

"We're in no hurry!" yelled Coach RJ.

Big Ant missed both free throws.

The coach yelled, "Pressure the ball!"

As the clock trickled down, the other team struggled to get past half court. Blake stole the ball with twenty seconds left.

"One shot!" shouted Coach RJ.

Blake penetrated and tossed the ball in the air. When Big Ant caught it and dunked it in midair, the buzzer sounded.

"Yea, man!" as people ran onto the court.

Jewels jumped into Blake's arms while Jessica stood waiting to embrace him.

She thought, "Who is she?"

Story 16
What Happens
In Major City

Part 1: Find

Pickney was hanging pictures of her and Man in her apartment when she heard a knock on her door. She checked the peephole and opened it, smiling. When Will and The Bass Boys came in, Tucker ran into Big Ant's arms. After a long hug from Blake, she walked them to the living room where Will and Big Ant flopped on the sofa. Fish parked himself beside the love seat where Blake sat skimming through family photos.

While lazing in her accent chair, Pickney told him about each one before asking, "So, what are your plans?"

Blake said, "We don't start college until next semester, so we're here for Will."

"What about Jessica, man?"

"And for me, too," he said.

"I'm Will by the way," and he stood to shake her hand.

Pickney asked, "What makes you so eager to see the city?"

"The Crazy Cupid Machine."

Blake said, "The Mowing Man has it."

"So, our plan is to find him," said Fish.

"What if you don't?"

"Then, we'll call Jessica to see if she knows any hot college girls that want to hang out."

"No, we have to find him," said Will, looking into their eyes. "That machine could be worth millions."

Part 2: Millionaire

Will and The Bass Boys split up into twos to cover every business they assumed bought the machine first. Will and Blake went east while Big Ant and Fish drove to the west side. After finding out nothing, the two Bass Boys met up with Will and Blake who were coming from the south side of the city. When Will asked them if they had been north, they shook their heads and suggested they go together before breaking at Jessica's apartment near the college campus.

"Alright, last one," said Will, looking up at the tall building.

"Man, there's got to be a million dollars hidden somewhere in there."

Blake said, "Anthony, you and Fish stay outside."

As they eased past the front desk and onto the elevator, Big Ant and Fish tried counting the number of floors from the sidewalk.

Meanwhile inside, Will and Blake exited onto the second floor to check the directory.

"Alright," said Will, "I think we go here," pointing to the seventh floor.

A man was walking by counting money when Blake asked, "Do you think he's a millionaire?"

"Nah, probably just a bonus," said Will, entering the elevator.

Meanwhile on the seventh floor, the owner of the company was in a meeting.

He said, "We need something different. Something that can appeal to a younger audience. What are teenagers into nowadays?"

"Sex," someone said.

"May be a bit risky," said the owner, "but it's the truth. I love it! Now, what can we make that caters to their craving for sex?"

Will and Blake walked in.

"Sorry to interrupt," said Will, "but did an older Black man sell a machine to you guys?"

The owner said, "What kind of machine?"

"A love machine," said Blake.

"That's it!" said the owner, jumping up out his seat.

He demanded his committee to organize the paperwork for the boys to sign before shaking their hands. The owner walked Will to a vacant chair and offered him some snuff from his near empty can. Will stuffed some in his mouth with his feet up while Blake was introducing himself to the committee.

"Are you ready to be a millionaire?"

"I've been ready."

The owner said, "So, then where is it?"

"The Mowing Man has it."

"Then, get out my conference room! Hey, *you*," pointing at a member of his committee, "find me The Mowing Man!"

Part 3: Commit

Jessica asked, "So, how are you guys going to find The Mowing Man?"

"There's only one way to find him," said Blake, looking through her fridge.

"But it's been so long," said Fish, eating at the table. "He could be back in Venoa Beach."

"Who would want to go back to Venoa Beach after a taste of the big city life?" asked Will.

"He's got a point, man."

Blake made himself a sandwich while the rest of the boys went outside by Big Ant's SUV to blast music. Fish was eyeing the female neighbors, Will was two stepping, and Big Ant was bobbing his head to the beat. When Pretty Patty drove up waving, Fish wheeled himself over to her for conversation.

He said, "It's decent of you to room with Jessica after all you two been through."

"She was always in my heart," said Pretty Patty, eyeing Will.

Meanwhile, inside, Blake and Jessica were arguing.

"What's it going to take for you to fully commit to me?!" Jessica asked after skimming through his phone.

"Jewels is just a friend!"

"The way she jumped in your arms at the game says she's interested in more! Believe me, I'm a girl!"

"If you want me to delete her number, then no more parties, only intimate gatherings," said Blake.

"Deal."

Part 4: Deal

Will finished tattooing over Blake's heart.

"Is that someone's name?" asked Rosemary.

"His name was Haywood," said Blake.

Fish and Big Ant admired theirs in the mirror, having the same exact design as Blake. As the four boys were hanging out in Rosemary's new shop, an old Black man walked in with a broom. After he was avoided by people roaming the large mall because of his smell, Rosemary greeted him with a hug.

The old man was sweeping the shop when Fish asked, "Can't you just clean yourself?"

Rosemary said, "I could, but he and I made a deal."

"I sweep, she feeds," said the old man.

"He's homeless, so I pay for his lunch."

Will said, "Then, he might know The Mowing Man."

"Oh," said the old man, "there was a guy who used to drop-in at the shelter I was at a while ago, who could never wash the grass stains out his clothes. He used to hand out slurpees to the wealthy in exchange for a steak dinner to feel like he had his old life back. If you ask me, he was making deals with the devil."

"Man, that's got to be him."

"Where's the shelter at?" asked Fish.

"City Street."

Blake exclaimed, "Let's go, guys."

"Be safe," said the old man. "Be *safe*."

Part 5: Safer

During lunch hours, when the dining area for the homeless was open to the public, Will and The Bass Boys entered the shelter after being searched by security guards. Pretending to be as starved as the old man at Rosemary's Tattoo Parlor was on a regular basis, they stood in line to be fed. The boys were served a fair share and sat at separate tables to talk to as many men about The Mowing Man as possible.

Big Ant was talking to one who said, "I know him because he used to tote that machine around in a wagon."

"Man, do you know where he is or could be?"

"Wherever he is," said the man, "he's safer than he would be in here."

"What about the security guards, man?"

"They don't stand a chance against an angry man with nothing to lose."

Big Ant called over his friends.

"Man, he thinks he's somewhere safe."

Fish said, "What's safer than a homeless shelter?"

"Everywhere else," said the man.

Will asked, "What's the safest place in city?"

"He used to sing at Crystal's downtown on open mic night. She might know where he is."

Part 6: Song

There were about six tables surrounding the stage where a local musician played, singing his heart out for a large payout. With every seat taken at the bar, Will and The Bass Boys picked a table right under the dim light to see who was coming and going.

"Which one's Crystal?" Fish asked the waitress.

"Crystal doesn't work tonight."

Blake asked, "So, then who's in charge?"

"Me," she said, smiling. "I'm a waitress, bartender, and manager all wrapped in one."

"Then, maybe you can help us," said Will.

"It would be my pleasure."

"Does an old Black man come here often to sing?"

"There's one," said the woman. "He calls himself The Mowing Man, and always sings the same song he said was his *wife's* favorite."

Fish asked, "When was the last time he was here?"

"A while ago," she said.

"Do you know where he is, or where he hangs out?" Blake asked.

The women said, "City Park."

The boys slapped fives as she walked away, giving them more time to decide on their order. With no intention of eating, Will and The Bass Boys asked the musician for the mic. As they started to sing, people started to leave. The woman in charge noticed and chased them off stage before they rushed out.

Part 7: Chase

Children chased each other around while their parents followed the paved trail chatting in the sun above City Park. Readers left space on the benches for those needing a break from jogging. Others with their laptops sat on the grass for a better signal. Will and The Bass Boys were roaming when the dropout spotted a homeless man sleeping in the shade.

"Wake him up," said Fish.

"Let him sleep, man."

Blake said, "This is urgent."

"I'll wake him," said Will, and he did.

Rubbing his eyes, he said, "Where does a bum like me get the money for a pair of decent shades? Collecting aluminum cans ain't going to cut it."

Fish said, "We have some questions for you."

"Shoot," said the homeless man.

"Have you seen an old Black man toting a machine around in a wagon?" asked Will.

"Nope," he said.

"We heard he hangs out here a lot," said Blake.

"What do they call him?"

They said, "The Mowing Man."

"Never heard of him. Now, go away."

The boys were turning their backs when the homeless man stood to stretch his arms and legs. As he was putting his backpack on, a nylon cup fell out of it.

Will turned around and shouted, "You do know him!"

The homeless man ran as Will and The Bass Boys chased him around the park. Big Ant was pushing Fish along when Will and Blake split up. They dodged the dog walkers and cut through the trees. When the homeless man tripped over his feet, Will jumped on his back as Blake was coming from the opposite direction.

"Tell us what you know," said Will, grabbing him by the collar.

"He's been trying to sell the machine to the wealthy, but no one will buy because they think it's stolen property!"

"Where is he?" asked Blake.

"I don't know!"

Will exclaimed, "You're lying again!"

"Check the bus station! That's where he panhandles the most, so he can get around the city."

Will let him go.

Part 8: Lie

Will and The Bass Boys sat inside the terminal.

"No sign of him, man."

Blake said, "Just keep an eye out."

"We've been waiting for an hour," said Fish.

As a driver stood outside skimming through his phone, Will said, "I'm going to ask."

To avoid being lied to again, the dropout bought a chocolate bar out a machine and smeared his shirt. After untying one of his braids to appear to be struggling to care for himself even more, Will approached him shaking an empty cup.

"I don't have any change," said the driver, sipping soda.

"I bet you get a lot of guys asking for money around here."

He said, "Police almost arrested one yesterday, but he complied, so they let him go."

"Do you remember what he looked like?"

"An older Black man with grass stains on his clothes who smiled without showing his teeth, as if he was lying about feeling happy enough to smile."

"Did he offer you a slurpee?"

"Oh, from his machine? Yea, but I turned him down. Too sweet for my taste buds."

"Where would you go if you were him?"

He said, "Theme parks."

Part 9: Sweet

Lady of Red was reading a book behind her register while Will and The Bass Boys toured her shop. With flowers at every turn, they basked in the sweet smell coming from the petals, comparing it to the voices of females worth their effort. After finishing her book, Lady of Red explained each flower's uniqueness and suggested she wrap some up for The Mowing Man.

"Men don't receive flowers," said Fish.

"For his wife," said Lady of Red. "Maybe they'll remind him of her."

"But he stole my machine!"

She said, "Please, be sweet to him."

"She's right, man."

"We don't even know where he is," said Will.

Blake said, "He's in the tourist area. That's where he would make the most money panhandling."

"Yea, man, who goes out of town without any money?"

"Then, let's go," Will said and headed for the door.

Lady of Red said, "Wait, aren't you forgetting something?"

She handed him the bouquet and hugged him before they left.

Part 10: Forget

Big Ant parked outside the gift shop.

"Let's just forget about it," said Will, shutting the door.

Blake said, "It's already dark out, so he should show up any minute."

Fish wheeled himself onto the sidewalk where they started to walk, blending in with tourists in the middle of exploring. They searched the hotel lobbies and restaurants and waited in parking lots with hopes he would appear.

They were back standing on the sidewalk when they overheard an older woman ask her husband, "Did you know that there's an abandoned amusement park over there, dear?"

"I'll never forget when it first opened," he said.

Meanwhile, The Mowing Man was on a carousel horse inside it, pretending to ride when Angel appeared.

"Come on, Elanor! I see you in the ol' wind!"

"The wind is unforgiving, si? When it blows, no one tells it to stop. It does not care what it knocks down. Now, Elanor, mi hombre, has forgiven."

The Mowing Man got off the horse, looked into his eyes, and asked, "What do you know about forgiveness?"

"I know it is much harder to forgive ourselves than it is others."

"I wish I could go back," said The Mowing Man, crying.

"What we have lost was only borrowed. The relationships that ended teach us, si? And so, we die with lessons in us and possessions around us, and we all know what's inside us is what counts."

As The Mowing Man poured kerosene over his head, Will and The Bass Boys appeared.

"What are you doing?!" shouted Will.

"Going to be with my Elanor! She forgave me!"

"You have to forget about her!"

The Mowing Man asked him, "Will you do the honors?" and handed him a cigarette lighter.

"Do it," said Blake.

Fish said, "You're one of us now."

"Haywood made you guys The Bass Boys. With me, we're The Bold Boys," he said while setting The Mowing Man on fire.

Meanwhile, two homeless city boys were watching.

As The Mowing Man burned alive, they asked, "Hey, who are you guys?"

Fish wheeled himself closer and looked them cold in the eyes and said, "*Venoans.*"

Author's Final Words

You miss as much out of life by living in fear as you would serving a life sentence.

"I believe that youth is spent well on the young because wisdom in your teens would be a lot less fun."

—Josh Kear

"I ain't a killer, but don't push me. Revenge is like the sweetest joy next to getting pussy."

—Tupac Shakur

"When the work you put in is realized, let yourself feel the pride but always stay humble and kind."

—Lori McKenna

www.ingramcontent.com/pod-product-compliance
Lightning Source LLC
Chambersburg PA
CBHW050029120726
47903CB00006B/1962